COMEBACK

Richard Stark

THE MYSTERIOUS PRESS

Published by Warner Books

A Time Warner Company

Mysterious Press books are published by Warner Books, Inc.,
1271 Avenue of the Americas, New York, NY 10020.

Visit our Web site at http://warnerbooks.com

A Time Warner Company

The Mysterious Press name and logo are registered trademarks of
Warner Books, Inc.
Printed in the United States of America
First printing: October 1997

10   9   8   7   6   5   4   3   2   1

Library of Congress Cataloging-in-Publication Data

Stark, Richard.
    Comeback / Richard Stark.
       p.   cm.
    ISBN 0-89296-661-0
    I. Title.
  PS3573.E9C66   1997
  823'.914—dc21   97-7019
                                                      CIP

Book design by Giorgetta Bell McRee

This is for Abby,
who said do it

The outcome you have waited for is assured.
Continue to persevere.
—Chinese Fortune Cookie

COMEBACK

ONE

1

When the angel opened the door, Parker stepped first past the threshold into the darkness of the cinder block corridor beneath the stage. A hymn filtered discordantly through the rough walls; thousands of voices, raggedly together. The angel said, "I'm not sure about this . . ."

"We are," Parker told him. Holding the door open with one splayed hand, he nodded back at Mackey and Liss, who slipped in quickly past him, carrying the duffel bags. Parker shut the metal fire door and pulled up on the bar to lock it again, while Liss stood his duffel on the floor with a muffled clank and loosened the loop of rope that closed the top. Mackey's duffel was full of other duffel bags, and for now stayed on his shoulder. Liss slid the rough canvas cloth of the bag down past the blunt metal barrels, then took out the three shotguns, giving one each to Parker and Mackey, then flipping the empty bag over his shoulder.

The angel blinked, watching. His heavy white robe and strapped-on feathery wings must have been hot, even in the air-conditioned arena; the white makeup on his face ran with perspiration, giving him the look of somebody who'd been dead a long time. Inside the costume and the makeup and the sweat, he was scared, with frightened pinpoint eyes. "There's too many guards," he said. His voice squeaked with the requirement that he keep it guarded and quiet. "Too much going on. We'll do it another time. A better time."

"We're set up now, Tom," Liss said. "You got nerves, that's all." He and Parker and Mackey had taken shells from their shirt pockets, broke open the shotguns, and were thumbing the shells into place.

"I don't want to do it now!" The angel's voice was more and more shrill, echoing around the echoes of the distant hymn. "We'll get caught!"

This amateur, this inside man, was Liss's pigeon; let Liss smooth his feathers. Parker saw Liss's jaw muscles set on the left side, where they worked. Liss didn't like his pigeon acting up in front of the string. He said, "Don't worry about it, okay? Lead the way."

But the angel wouldn't move. Blinking sweat out of his eyes, fidgeting his hands together as the limp wings moved on his back, he said, "We can't do it. I told somebody."

They all became very still. They looked at the angel, whose name was Tom Carmody. Liss said, "A woman?"

The angel looked ashamed. "Yes. I thought it was all right, but . . ."

"But what?"

"She's gone. She isn't at home. She isn't at work. Nobody knows where she is."

Parker said, "She's with this bunch? Your bunch?"

"No, she teaches at a special school for disturbed kids. They don't know where she is."

Mackey leaned his duffel bag against the wall. He said, "You live with her?"

"No. Not really. She has her own place." The angel was miserable, he was scared and embarrassed and unhappy. He was also an asshole. He said, "I don't know what she'll do."

Liss said, "Tom? You two have a fight? She mad at you? Maybe go to the cops?"

"No, no, nothing like that, she just disappeared. I don't *know* why."

Liss looked around at his partners. He'd

brought them into this, and now a decision had to be made. "What do you think?"

Parker said, "How much did he tell her? Everything—"

"Just a little!" the angel cried.

Parker looked at him. "Shut up." To the others he said, "Everything she wanted to know, that's how much. So she has the route in, she has a little idea what's going down inside, but not the route out. We're here, so if it's trouble, it's already trouble."

"That's right," Mackey said. "No point stopping."

Liss turned back to Carmody and gestured with the shotgun. "Lead the way."

"Please." Carmody spread his hands like a holy statue. "Please let's just call it off, it's just a mistake, it would be better to *burn* the rotten money than—"

Parker reached out and closed his left hand around Carmody's right thumb, bending the thumb in on itself, applying only the slightest pressure. Carmody's face turned almost as white as the makeup smeared on it, his knees bent, his mouth opened in a wide O. Parker said, "Shut up, now. You said your say. Now we walk to the money room."

Carmody tried to say something else, but Parker squeezed just a little bit harder, and no sound but a faint whimper came out of the angel's mouth. Obedient, wide-eyed, he turned, his sandals shuffling on the concrete, and they all walked together along the gently curving corridor, lit by widely spaced fluorescent tubes mounted on the ceiling. Parker and the angel looked like they were holding hands, flanked by the other two as they walked from light to light, the three big hard-boned men in dark clothing, carrying shotguns, all round the bedraggled angel, shoulders slumped beneath the useless wings.

The hymn-singing got louder as they progressed, more aggressive, ridding the world of evil by shouting at it. A side corridor went up to the left, and they paused there to look.

That corridor, tunnel-like, was dark and low-ceilinged, with a closed mesh gate at the end. Beyond the mesh were the bright field lights, washing the arena in a glare of white, so that from where Parker and the others stood it was impossible to make out exactly what was taking place on the artificial turf out there. A mass of people, their backs turned, all swaying so that the light glinted and shifted, harsh white bleaching out the colors, making the shadows blacker than black. Except for the rolling roar of the hymn, almost anything could have been going on out there; a political rally, a demolition derby, a football game. At one time or another, the arena had been used for all of those, but tonight the attraction that had brought twenty thousand souls to this domed arena in the American heartland was William Archibald and his Christian Crusade.

The hymn ended. The people shuffled and stirred, and the amplified fruity voice of Archibald himself sounded above and around and among them all as though speaking from a cloud: "Brothers! Sisters! Fellow mortals!"

"Come on," Parker said, and tugged gently on the thumb.

Tom Carmody's resistance was all used up. As the other two followed, he plodded along at Parker's side, shaking his head slowly. "I hate that bastard," he muttered, but in an exhausted way, without passion. "I hate his lying voice. I hate everything he does. I ought to *burn* the money, and him in it. Burn him in his own rotten piles of cash."

Parker tightened his grip on Carmody's bent thumb, just a little, just enough to bring him back to earth. "Where's the money room?"

"Ahead!" Pain and surprise were in Carmody's voice; he hadn't known he deserved punishment. "Just up ahead."

"Keep your mind on what we're doing."

They walked a little farther, the corridor constantly curving, appearing ahead of them, disappearing behind their backs, and then they came to a brown metal door on the interior side of the curve, with white block letters reading NO ADMITTANCE. Parker released the angel's thumb, and Carmody immediately closed his other hand around it, like one small animal comforting another. "Do it," Parker said, and prodded him in the side with the shotgun barrel, the blued metal poking into the white folds of the robe.

As the three armed men stood against the shadowed wall, Carmody stumbled forward and stood in front of the door. His left hand reluctantly released the aching thumb and pressed the button beside the door. He stood there blinking, the sharp fluorescent light above his head making him look more like a clown than an angel, and then a harsh voice sounded from the grid below the button: "Yes?"

"Hi, Harry. It's Tom Carmody." The angel's voice sounded almost normal; it hardly quavered at all.

"Hi, Tom," said the voice from the grid. "Come on in." A raspy buzzing sound came from the door.

Carmody pressed his non-painful hand to the door and it clicked open. Holding it that way, opening inward toward the corridor to the money room beneath the stands, he looked at Parker and said, "All right?"

Mackey moved forward to take the door. "You did fine," Parker said, and hammered the angel with the shotgun butt.

2

It began with a phone call. Parker didn't hear it ring, because he was out on the lake, in the rowboat, oars shipped, doing nothing, feeling the pulse of the water through the wood hull. Early May, this lake in northern New Jersey was still too cold to swim in, most of the vacation houses around its fringe still closed down, waiting for their owners to come back from the city when weather and water got a little warmer. Parker and Claire were among the few year-round residents, Claire establishing her presence in the community, Parker more aloof, being someone whose work let him stay at home for periods of time and then took him away sometimes. Claire was the one who made the home here, being Claire Willis because Parker had been Charles

Willis a long time ago, before they'd met. She liked the idea of reaching back into the world when they hadn't known one another, to make a link, throw a line back into the past.

Movement. He always reacted to movement, no matter how small, anywhere in his vision. This was three-quarters behind him, and when he turned his head it was Claire, at the dock, waving. The lawn stretched behind her up to the dark house. He lifted a hand, then rowed back, and as he stepped up onto the dock she said, "Man called. Pay phone. Says he'll call back in ten minutes." She looked at the slender watch on her slender wrist and corrected herself: "Six minutes."

"Did he give a name?"

"George Liss."

Parker frowned at that, and tied the boat to the stanchion, and they walked up to the house, she holding his wrist in her cool fingers. She said, "He seemed like he knew you."

"To a point," Parker said.

Parker and George Liss had never worked together, though they'd come close. Twice, they'd met on other guys' deals that hadn't panned out. He had no real opinion about George Liss, except he thought he probably wouldn't want to count on him if things turned sour.

The money situation at the moment was all

right, but not perfect. There was cash here and there, stowed away. He could wait for something that smelled good. Even in a world of electronic cash transfers and credit cards and money floating in cyberspace, there were still heists out there, waiting to be collected.

When the phone rang the second time, Parker was in the enclosed porch that faced the lawn and the lake and the boathouse, standing there, looking out. The day was overcast, and looked colder than it was. He picked up the phone on the third ring and said, "George?"

"I've got something." The voice slurred a little, making a furry sound in the phone lines.

Parker waited. George Liss could have a lot of things, including a need to turn someone else over to the law to take his place.

Liss said, "It's a little different, but it's profitable."

They were all different, and they were all supposed to be profitable, or you wouldn't do it. Parker waited.

Liss said, "You still there?"

"Yes."

"We could get together someplace, talk it over."

"Maybe."

"You want to know who else is aboard." And again Liss waited for Parker to say something, but again Parker had nothing to say, so finally Liss said, "Ed Mackey."

That was different. Ed Mackey was somebody Parker did know and had worked with. Ed Mackey was solid. Parker said, "Who else?"

"It only takes three."

Even better. The fewer the people, the fewer the complications, and the more the profit. Parker said, "Where and when?"

They came together first in the parking lot of a lobster restaurant on Route 1 just south of Auburn, Maine, a place where a couple of rental cars from Boston's Logan Airport wouldn't look out of place. Parker left his Impala and crisscrossed through the parked cars to the Century Regal where Ed Mackey, blunt and taciturn, sat at the wheel with his girlfriend Brenda beside him and George Liss in the back seat. Parker joined Liss, a tall, narrow, black-haired man with a long chin, who nodded at him and smiled with the side of his mouth where the nerves and muscles still worked, and said, "Have a good flight?"

This wasn't a sensible question. Parker said, "Tell me about it."

"It's a stadium," Ed Mackey said, half-turning in the front seat, knees pointed at Brenda as he looked back at Parker. "Usual stadium security. Twenty thousand civilians inside."

Parker shook his head. "All you walk out with," he said, "is credit card receipts."

"Not this one," Liss said, and the left side of his face smiled more broadly. A sharpened spoon handle had laid open the right side, in a prison in Wyoming, eleven years ago. A plastic surgeon had made the scars disappear, but nothing could make that side of his face move again, ever. Around civilians, Liss usually tried to keep himself turned partially away, showing only the profile that worked, but among fellow mechanics he didn't worry about it. With the slight slurring that made his words always sound just a little odd, he said, "This one is all cash. Paid at the door."

"They call it love offerings," Mackey said, deadpan.

Parker tried to read Mackey's face. "Love offerings? What kind of stadium is this?"

Liss explained, "The stadium's the usual. The *attraction's* a guy named William Archibald. A TV preacher, you know those guys? Evangelists."

"I thought they were all in jail," Parker said.

"The woods are full of them," Liss said, and Mackey added, "Mostly the back woods."

Parker said, "He's preaching at this stadium, is that it?"

"To make a movie," Mackey said, "and show it on the TV later."

"The people walking in," Liss said, moving his hands around in the space between himself and Parker, "they put down a twenty-dollar love offering, every one of them. No exceptions. Twenty thousand people."

Brenda spoke for the first time: "Four hundred thousand dollars," she said in her husky voice, rolling her full lips around the words.

"Brenda does my math for me," Mackey said.

"Plus," Liss said, "they got these barrels up front by the stage, you get inspired along the way, you want to help the preacher spread the word on the TV, you can go up and toss whatever money you want in the barrel."

"On TV," Mackey said. "On the big screen up behind the preacher. I seen it work, Parker, it's like hypnotizing. These people *love* to see themselves on that big screen, walkin right up there, tossin their cash in the old barrel. Then a month later, they're at home, TV on, there they are again. Live the moment twice. The day you gave the rent money to God."

"We figure," Liss said, "that doubles the take."

Brenda opened her mouth, but before she could say anything Mackey pointed at her and said, "Brenda. He can work it out."

Parker said, "There's going to be more than the usual security, if it's all cash."

"Archibald has his own people," Liss agreed.

"But we got a guy on the inside. That's what made it start to happen."

"Not one of us," Parker said.

"Not for a minute," Mackey said.

"He works for the preacher," Liss said. "And now he's mad at him."

"Greedy? Wants a bigger slice?"

"Just the reverse," Liss said, and half his face laughed. "Ol' Tom got religion."

"Just tell it to me," Parker said.

Mackey patted the top of the seatback, as though calming a horse. "It's a good story, Parker," he said. "Wait for it."

People had to tell their stories their own way, with all the pointless extras. "Go ahead," Parker said, and sat back to wait it out.

Liss said, "I had twenty-nine months' parole last time I got out. It was easier, just hang around and do it, then have a paper out on me the rest of my life. This guy Archibald, one of his scams is, his people volunteer to give this *counseling* to ex-cons. It's all crap and everybody knows it, it's just to find new suckers, and to get some kinda tax break."

"A cash business," Parker said. "He's doin okay with taxes anyway."

"Oh, you know he is. But William Archibald, he's one of those guys, the more you give him to drink, the thirstier he gets. So I drew this guy

Tom Carmody to be my counselor, once a week he'd come around the place I was living, and then when he'd fill out the sheet, that meant I didn't have to go in to the parole office. A good deal for everybody. And after the first few weeks, we pretty much come clean with each other, and after that we'd just watch basketball on the tube or something, or have a beer around the corner. I mean, he knew what I was and no problem, and I knew what scam *he* was on, so we just got on with life. Except sometimes he'd go on crusades, and—"

Parker said, "Crusades?"

"When Archibald takes his show on the road," Liss explained. "Rents a hall, a movie house, a stadium, someplace big, does his act three, four times, brings in a couple mil, takes it all home again. Tom was one of the staff guys he brought along on these things, so then I'd get some gung ho trainee from the office instead, and I'd have to be real serious and rehabilitated and grateful as hell to Jesus and all this shit, and then when Tom came back we'd laugh about it. Only, then, about the last six months—yeah, two years we're dealing bullshit and we both knew it, and then the last six months he began to change it all around. Not trying to reform *me* or nothing. It was Archibald he got agitated about."

Brenda spoke again, this time drily: "He noticed Mister Archibald was insincere."

"He got hung up on the money," Liss said. "How Archibald takes all the suckers for all this money, and it doesn't go anywhere good. I dunno, Parker, it wasn't the *scam* that got ol' Tom riled up, it still isn't. It's what happens with the money *after* Archibald trims the rubes. He'd talk about all the good that money could do, you know, feed the homeless and house the hungry and all this, and then he wanted to know was there any way I knew that he could *get* a bunch of that cash. Not for himself, you see, but to do good works with it."

Parker said, "It was his idea?"

"Absolutely. The guy's a civilian, I only know him two years, and he's tied to the parole board. Am I gonna say, 'Hey, Tom, let's pull a number'? No way."

"But you went along."

Liss shook his head. "Not at first. One of the few big words I know is *entrapment*. So at first I'd just nod and say well, that's a real bitch, Tom, and all this. And when he finally came out with it—'Hey, George, let's do it together, you with your expert background and me with my inside information'—I told him no, I told him I'm retired, it isn't I'm reformed I just don't want to go back inside. Which was almost the truth, by the way."

Parker nodded. For a lot of people, that was almost the truth almost all the time.

"Also," Liss said, "I told him I didn't much care where money went that didn't come to me, whether this money fed Archibald or fed some other people made no difference to me, and he said he understood. He understood for me it would be more of a business proposition. So he suggested we split fifty-fifty, and I'd put my share in my pocket and he'd give his to the poor."

"Us poor," Mackey said.

Parker knew what Mackey meant. Glancing at him, "If," he said.

"Naturally."

Liss went on, saying, "Finally I said I'd pass him on to somebody who was still active in the game, but he said no, he wouldn't trust anybody but me, so then I figured I could take the chance. If he was out to trap somebody for the law, he wouldn't care who he brought in, right? He'd let me pass him on to somebody else, work his number just as good. Since he didn't do that, then he probably wasn't pulling anything. So then we started to get kind of serious, talking it over, him giving me the details about the money, and I saw how maybe it could be done. And here we are."

Parker said, "And the theory is, the inside guy takes half, and we split the other half. However many of us it is doing the thing."

"That's the theory."

"Does he buy it?" Parker shook his head, rejecting his own question, rephrasing it: "What I mean, does he believe it?"

"That he'll get his half?" Liss did his lopsided smile. "That's the big question, isn't it? He's kind of hard to read since he changed, you know. Used to be, he was an easygoing guy, now he's all tensed up. Relaxed guys are harder to fool, but tensed-up guys are harder to read."

"Anyway, Parker," Mackey said, "what's he gonna do if he *doesn't* believe it? We're the takers, not him. Is he gonna take it from the takers? No way."

Parker ignored that. He said to Liss, "How many parole guys does this fella have beer with?"

Liss half-frowned; that face of his took some getting used to. He said, "You mean, he puts together a backup crew to take it away after we get it? But what's the point, Parker? If he's afraid *we're* gonna cut him out, what's he gonna do about the second crew? Come up with a third?"

"What I think it is," Mackey said, "I think the guy bought his own story. He's not buying from us, he's buying from himself."

Parker said to Mackey, "You meet this wonder?"

"Not yet."

"That can be arranged," Liss said. "Easiest thing there is. I'll call him tonight, say we're—"

"No," Parker said. "You say he goes out with this preacher on his crusades. When's the next one?"

"Couple weeks. I figured that's when we could pull it."

"No. Where they gonna be? The whole tour."

Liss's face went out of whack again. He said, "Beats me. I guess I could find out."

"Good," Parker said. "Then somewhere along the way, without any invitations or planning or setting things up, we're there, and we say hello. Mackey and me."

"And Brenda," Mackey said.

Parker looked at Brenda. "Naturally," he said.

3

In a not-very-good restaurant in St. Louis, with old bored waiters and old-fashioned dark red-and-brown decor, Parker and Mackey and Brenda ate dinner, taking their time over it. Liss had said he'd get the pigeon here between eight and ten, and it was already nine-thirty. "I gotta go to the john again," Brenda said, fooling with her coffee cup, "but I know, the minute I leave the table, they're gonna walk in."

"Then do it," Mackey told her. "I'd like to see *something* make them walk in."

"Only for you," she said, and left the table, and a minute later Liss walked in with a sandy-haired nervous-looking guy in his late twenties, wearing tan slacks and a plaid shirt.

"There, you see," Mackey said. "That's why I keep Brenda around. She's magic."

Parker said nothing. He already knew why Mackey kept Brenda around—she was his brains—and his interest was in the guy over there with Liss. And also with whoever might come into the restaurant next.

Which was nobody. If Carmody was being watched, it was a very long leash. Watchers couldn't have been planted in the place ahead of time, because Liss wouldn't have told Tom where they were going until they got here. "This looks like a good place, Tom. I'm ready for dinner, how about you?"

And why would a watcher wait outside, when the whole point of keeping an eye on your bait was to see who came around and what happened? So Tom was not under observation. Which didn't mean he wasn't a Judas goat, only that, if he was, they were letting him float on his own. Not important to them, in other words, or not yet. Not until he starts to come home with somebody.

Liss had seated himself at the table in a chair where he could give the doddering waiter his good side, about which the waiter cared nothing. Tom Carmody, across from Liss, was quiet, low-key, ordering as though he didn't care if he ate or not, then sitting there in a funk. Liss gave him a minute or two of cheery conversation and then ate rolls instead.

Brenda came back to the table and Mackey said, "Your magic worked."

"So I see."

While Mackey signaled to the waiter for the check, Brenda studied the guy sitting over there with Liss. Mackey repeated his hand gesture at the waiter—signing his name in the air—then turned back to Brenda to say, "What do you think?"

"He's too gloomy."

"I don't want you to date him, honey."

"I don't want you to date him, either," she said. "That's what I mean, he's too gloomy."

Parker listened, while across the way Liss and Carmody got their salads. Liss tucked in, while Carmody pushed the lettuce and tomato slice around in the shallow bowl.

Meantime, Mackey said, "Explain yourself," and Brenda said, "He already gave up. Look at him, Ed. He doesn't care if anything good happens or not. You know what a guy like that does when there's trouble? He lies down."

"Good," Mackey said. "He'll give us traction."

The waiter brought the check then, and stood around as Mackey brought out his wallet and, despite the hand signal, paid in cash. While he did that, Brenda said to Parker, "How's Claire?"

Unlike Mackey, Parker didn't bring his woman to work. "She's fine," he said.

"Will I be seeing her?"

"I don't think so."

Mackey left a little tip, and said, "Let's go look at our boy up close."

Parker let Mackey and Brenda go first; they were better at the social niceties, like pretending to be happily surprised at the sight of Liss sitting there: "George! How you doing, old son?"

"Hello, Ed! How are you? And Brenda!" Liss rose, shaking Mackey's hand, kissing Brenda's cheek, giving Parker a bright-eyed look of non-recognition.

Mackey said, "George Liss, here's a pal of ours, Jack Grant."

"How you doing, Jack?" Liss said, grinning, extending his hand.

"Fine," Parker said, shaking the hand briefly. Play-acting wasn't what he did best.

On the other hand, Liss was having a good time. "And this is a pal of *mine*," he announced, with a big wave at the pigeon. "Tom Carmody. Tom, this is Ed and Brenda Fawcett, and a pal of theirs."

Tom Carmody had been raised as a mannerly boy; he got to his feet and managed a smile at Brenda, with his how-do-you-dos. Mackey squeezed Carmody's hand, grinning hard at him, saying, "I'm a salesman, Tom, but I guess you can see that. Most people pipe me right away. You I don't get, though. You teach?"

"Not exactly." Carmody was clearly uncomfortable at having to explain himself. "I'm in rehabilitation," he said.

Mackey did a good job of misunderstanding. Looking concerned, he said, "Hey, I'm sorry. Whatcha rehabilitating from?"

"No, I'm—I—" Carmody's confusion made him blush. He finally managed to get it out: "I work for a preacher. We do rehabilitation work for, uh, people."

"Well, that's fine," Mackey told him. "There's a lotta people *need* that stuff." With a big jokey grin he said, "What about old George here? You gonna rehabilitate him?"

Carmody began to stumble and stutter all over himself again, but this time Liss came to his rescue, saying, "Not me. I'm a hopeless case."

"Us honest citizens shouldn't be seen with the likes of you," Mackey said, and whacked Liss playfully on the arm. "See you around, George."

Everybody said good-bye, Carmody sat down with obvious relief, and Parker and Mackey and Brenda went out to the parking lot, where Mackey had a laughing fit, leaning over the hood of their car. When he got himself under control he said, "That was touching, Parker. Do you know that? He didn't wanna blow the gaff on George being on parole. I call that touching."

"He's a very straight citizen," Parker agreed.

Mackey leaned against the car, wiping his eyes, and said to Brenda, "Well? What do you think? Still too gloomy?"

"I think you can take a chance," she said. "If everything else is okay. If Parker's going in."

"Yeah?" Mackey was interested. "How come the change of heart?"

"He isn't a liar," Brenda said. "He isn't trapping anybody, or double-crossing anybody, or anything like that, because that fella couldn't lie about what *time* it is without the whole thing showing on his face."

"Well, that's true." Mackey nodded, thinking it over, then grinned again and looked at Parker. "Ever work with a guy on *that* recommendation before? He can't tell a lie. Parker, we're signing on with George Washington."

4

They waited in the parking lot, and when Carmody came out with Liss half an hour later he stopped dead at the sight of them. Eyes round, he stared off toward the street for rescue, but before he could do anything foolish Liss took his elbow and said, reassuringly, "It's okay, Tom. This means they like you."

"What? What?"

Gently, Liss explained: "These are the people gonna help us, Tom. They wanted to see you first, see what they thought. If they figured you were okay, they'd wait here until we came out. And here they are."

"You mean, the, the—"

Mackey said, "That's right, Tom. The reverend's millions."

27

Startled, Carmody said, "Not millions!"

"I know, I know." Mackey grinned at himself. "I was just exaggerating, Tom, it's a bad habit I got. The number's four hundred grand, am I right? Two for us, two for you."

"Approximately," Carmody said.

Mackey spread his hands, looking at Liss. "How can we not love this guy, George?" he asked. "He doesn't want to mislead us or anything."

Parker said, "Carmody, you'll give George a list of the places where your preacher's going to be doing his thing the next four or five months."

Carmody said, "That long? I was hoping—"

"Maybe we'll do it next week," Parker told him, although he knew they wouldn't. "Maybe not till later. We'll do it when we got the right place, the right circumstances. You don't want any risk, right?"

"That's right," Carmody said. He stared at Parker like an antelope looking at a lion. "Mr. uh, Grant, is it?"

"Yeah."

"I never did anything like—"

"We know," Parker said. "George told us what your idea is. You want to do good."

"Whereas," Mackey said, "*we* want to do well."

Ignoring that, Parker said to Carmody, "If

something goes wrong, the cops won't ask you what your motive was. You see what I mean?"

"Absolutely," Carmody said.

"So we'll pick the right time, the right place, the right circumstances," Parker told him. "We'll decide when it's safe to make our move. And then we'll say to you, *now.*"

5

The money room was long, low-ceilinged and windowless. There were bright fluorescent lights in the ceiling, the walls were off-white plasterboard, and a pale gray industrial carpet was on the floor, but even with all that lightness and brightness the place had the feeling of being a cave or a tunnel, far underground. Air conditioning produced a flat dry atmosphere, in which sounds became muffled and small. The hymn-singing could not be heard in here.

Parker and Liss and Mackey came into the room fast, ski masks on their faces, the shotguns pointing outward, slightly over the occupants' heads, the blued-steel barrels moving back and forth as though looking for a target. Liss cried out, "Everybody stop! Stop now! Hands on desks! *You!* You'll die!"

The fat man with the black necktie stopped reaching for the phone. He and the other five people in the room all became very still. Three of them—the fat man and two middle-aged women, all seated at desks with open ledgers and calculators and video terminals—were employees of the arena, and would calm down when they stopped to remember it wasn't their money in any case. The other three, all slender short-haired young men in dark slacks and white shirts and narrow ties, were Reverend Archibald's people, and might take a robbery more personally.

These three had all been on their feet, standing around the long tables piled with money, still only partially counted. Now they all stood bent slightly forward, palms flat against the counting table as their eyes darted around, glancing quickly at one another, at the money, at the shotguns, at the lights and the floor and everything in the room. All three were thinking about trying something, even against the guns.

Mackey stepped forward toward the money table, keeping to the side so he didn't block Parker's and Liss's aim. He was jittery on his feet and bunching his shoulders up and down, giving them all kinds of body language about how wrought-up he was. His voice loud and ragged, full of tension, he yelled, "You three! Get away from the money!"

They stared at him, not moving. Mackey shook the shotgun in both hands. He bobbed on his feet. He yelled, "I gotta blow one of you bastards away! I gotta! So *move!*"

Liss angrily yelled, "Don't get blood on the money!"

"Move away!" Mackey screamed at the three. "Move away!"

Now finally one of them found voice. Frightened, gasping through the words, he said, "What do you want to shoot us for?"

Parker stepped forward. "Ed, don't do it," he said. "Not unless they give you a reason."

Mackey jittered forward close enough to touch the shotgun barrel against the white shirtsleeve of the one who'd spoken. "Give me a reason," he begged. "Give me a reason."

Parker, as though he wanted to calm Mackey down as much as anybody, said to the trio, "Down on the floor. Right where you are. On your backs. Ed won't shoot unless you're stupid."

The three went down fast, and lay blinking up at the ceiling. Like upended turtles, they felt more exposed and helpless on their backs than if Parker had let them lie face down, where they could have felt hidden and coiled. Between their position on the floor there and Mackey's apparent blood-hunger, they wouldn't be causing any trouble after all.

Parker had taken the bag of duffel bags from Mackey on the way in, to leave Mackey's arms free for when he went into his act. Now Parker turned to the two women seated at their desks, trying to be invisible, and tossed the duffel at them. "Take the bags out and fill them. The faster you do it, the sooner we're out of here."

The women hurried across to the money table, stepping over the supine men. Awkward with haste, they stuffed money into the gray canvas bags, while Mackey kept pacing around, muttering to himself and rubbing the top of his head. Liss stood near the door, the shotgun in his hands moving in arcs, like a surveillance camera. Parker went past him and back out to the small anteroom, where they'd left Carmody, who was still out, lying on the floor where they'd dragged him. He went back inside and Mackey was fidgeting back and forth, pointing his gun at the men on the floor and mumbling incomprehensible things, while the two women kept sneaking terrified looks at him and filling the duffel bags as rapidly as they possibly could.

Parker went around the room, unsnapping the phone cords connecting all the phones to their jacks, then bringing the phone cords over to the money table and stuffing them into a bag that was already half full.

Liss said to the fat man, "You can make that important call now."

The fat man was doing dignity; he sat, unmoving, head bent forward, gazing at a spot on the desk midway between his splayed-out hands. He pretended Liss hadn't spoken.

They'd brought six bags, but it only took five for all the money. "Give me the empty one," Parker told the women as they loaded the last of the cash, and they did. While he moved the duffels two at a time out to the anteroom, Liss told the people, "You'll stay in here a while. Ed's gonna hang around outside the door, hoping to shoot somebody. I don't know how long it's gonna take Jack and me to get him to leave, so don't be in any hurry to go anywhere."

Liss then joined Parker and the money in the anteroom, while Mackey raved at the people a while on his own. Looking down at Carmody, some dried blood on the side of the fellow's head looking fake against the angel makeup, Liss said, "Is he gonna hold?"

Parker had already put his shotgun in the empty duffel bag. Holding it open for Liss's weapon, he said, "He'll hold."

"I'm the one he could identify," Liss said. He

didn't put the shotgun in the duffel. He said, "I'm the one exposed if he breaks."

"If you kill him," Parker said, "they'll know he was the inside man. They'll look at who he knew, through that parole scam. They'll get to you for sure."

Liss thought about that. Mackey came out, shutting the door, and looked at them. "Something?"

"No," Liss said, and put his shotgun in the bag.

Mackey put his weapon with the others and said, "They'll stay in there a while. They'll stay in there until their pants dry." Then they tossed their ski masks into the bag with the guns, and left, each carrying two bags, Mackey carrying the heavier one with the guns.

Back where they'd come into the building, Parker cautiously opened the door and looked out. The parking lot was full of cars and empty of people. This was why they'd given up the idea of going for the money outside in the barrels. They would have had to wait until the crusade finished and everybody was out and moving. This way was cleaner and simpler.

The three moved quickly across the asphalt lot through the cars. It was a bright sunny fall day, temperature in the fifties, air very crisp and clear. They seemed to shimmy and disappear as they moved through the varicolored parked cars.

At the far end of the parking lot, five days ago, a construction company trailer had been set up here, wheeled in behind a semi cab, then chocked up and the perimeter beneath closed with concrete blocks. A sign on the side of the trailer read, in large blue letters on a white ground, MORAN CONSTRUCTION, SITE MANAGER'S OFFICE.

This was a legitimate trailer from a legitimate construction company, now bankrupt and shut down, but its assets not yet sold. The trailer had been stolen from the company's yard, using a cab that also belonged to the company. Once it was in position here, Mackey had hooked up the electric lines to a nearby power pole, and then they'd just left the thing alone. Archibald's crusade hadn't even been in this state when they'd moved the trailer into position. Such trailers are so often to be found in distant corners of large public parking areas that nobody looks twice at them. This one had been left undisturbed for five days.

Now, Parker did the combination on the padlock on the door and climbed up and in, followed by Liss and then by Mackey. They entered a cramped office, with desk and chair on one side and narrow hard sofa on the other, on and around which they dumped the duffel bags. To the right of the office was the john, complete with a very narrow shower—the trailer con-

tained its own water supply and waste storage—
and to the left was a compact living room, with
built-in sofas, a bookcase full of magazines and
paperbacks, and a small black-and-white television set. Beyond the living room was a galley-type
kitchen; five days ago, they'd stocked that with
beer and soda and canned food.

There was a small sliding window in the entry
door, covered on the inside by a stretched-tight
translucent plastic curtain. Once they were inside, Parker removed that curtain, unlatched the
window, slid the openable half out of the way,
reached out, and reattached the padlock to the
hasp on the door, locking them in. Then he slid
the window shut, latched it, and put the curtain
back in place.

Mackey came in from the kitchen with three
cans of beer. Distributing them, he said, "Parker,
I like this. It's very good. This is the most comfortable escape from a heist I ever made."

"Bad news to be running around out there
now," Parker said.

"You know it." Mackey popped open his beer.
"To a life of ease," he said.

Liss knocked back about half his beer, but still
looked troubled. "Now," he said, "all Tom has to
do is not make me sorry he's still alive."

6

It was a mess in the parking lot for a couple hours. Police cars and police lab vans blocked the aisles. An ambulance came and went, yowling, most likely dealing with Tom Carmody. Long tables were set up near the main arena entrance, where clerical cops processed the crusade's attendees, taking their IDs and giving them a few quick questions each, as the former crusade audience stood in long nervous patient lines. More cops searched every car before permitting it to be driven away. Twenty thousand people; every one of them given personal attention. It took a while.

Twice in the course of the afternoon, cops came over to the construction trailer to fiddle with the padlock and test the door to be sure it was locked and then knock on it, just in case. The second one did even more, walking all around the trailer to see if there was any other way in, then trying to look in through the three windows; the one in the door leading to the office, the large one in the living room through which Parker and Mackey and Liss occasionally watched the action outside, and the small high one in the john. But they were all covered by the translucent plastic curtains, so he gave up, and contented himself with copying down the Moran Construction Company phone number from the sign on the trailer's side. He wouldn't get much satisfaction if he actually dialed that number. *Out of service,* most likely.

The cops were nowhere near finished when it started to get dark, so three floodlight trucks were brought in and parked strategically to drench the area in light. Even at the fringe of the action, where Parker and the other two waited, there was plenty of illumination. It spilled into the trailer, giving them all the light they needed, softening into a pale coral color as if filtered through the curtains.

In that soft illumination, Parker and Mackey and Liss sat around the desk in the office and counted the money, which came to three hundred ninety-eight thousand, five hundred eighty dollars, all in fives and tens and twenties, and even some wrinkled singles. About as traceable as a drop of water.

After that, they mostly watched television, with the sound very low. Which meant they mostly watched other angles of what was going on outside. The half-million-dollar robbery at the arena—whether the exaggeration was Archibald's, the cops', or the television people's, was hard to guess—was the biggest event in this town since the last Rolling Stones farewell tour.

Around nine o'clock, Mackey moved the curtain slightly at the corner of the living room window, looked out, and said, "Parker, they're gonna still be here tomorrow morning."

The idea was, Brenda was expected at six in the morning. She'd drive by in a station wagon they'd promoted earlier, and if things seemed all right she'd come on into the parking area, they'd switch the goods, set the fuse on the bomb, and take off. (The only way to be sure they wouldn't leave incriminating evidence in the trailer was to blow it up.) But now Mackey, shaking his head as he looked out the window, said, "When Brenda gets here, she's gonna have to check in with the cops."

"They'll be gone," Parker said. "You're just getting antsy."

"And that's the truth," Mackey agreed, moving away from the window, sitting down again. "I never lived inside a tin can before," he explained. "Now I know how minestrone feels."

"How does Tom Carmody feel," Liss said tensely, "that's all I want to know."

Parker said, "He's got a concussion. He'll come out of it tomorrow groggy. They won't lean on him very hard, not right away. By the time they're really looking him over, he won't be nervous any more."

"Tom," Liss said, "will *always* be nervous."

Parker shrugged. "So will you, I guess."

Mackey leaned back, fingers laced behind his head, aggressive grin on his face. "Snowbound with my pals," he said. "Everybody getting along. No problems. From here on in, everything's gravy."

7

A flat metallic *click* woke Parker. He opened his eyes and in the darkness saw the dull glint of the shotgun barrels a foot from his face. Beyond them, Liss's eyes stood out, the whites luminous, as though lit from within.

Making a hoarse scared rale in his throat, Liss pulled the second trigger, and that *click* sounded again as Parker kicked him in the chest. Liss bounced backward into the wall, and Parker's left hand went up and closed around the barrels, yanking the shotgun away. Grasping the barrels with both hands, he surged up from the sofa and lunged the shotgun forward, the butt smashing into Liss's face.

"Hey! What the hell?" Mackey came boiling up from the other sofa, getting in Parker's way, the two of them stumbling around in the cramped space as Liss fell to the floor, then crawled quickly through the doorway into the other room.

"It's *Liss*," Parker said, pushing Mackey away. "Wanting it all."

"Son of a bitch."

Parker went to one knee, felt under the sofa cushion, came out with just one of the shells. Getting to his feet, he broke the shotgun as he went through the doorway. The exit door stood open. Thumbing in the shell, slapping the shotgun shut, Parker crossed to see Liss out there, hesitating over the three duffel bags.

They'd each crammed their third of the take into one of the bags, and Liss had moved all three outside before turning to rid himself of his partners: one barrel into Parker, then quickly one into Mackey, all of them together in the narrow room. If Parker hadn't quietly emptied the three shotguns earlier tonight, one time when he had gone to the john and the other two were watching television, he and Mackey would be dead.

Liss had thought he might grab one or more of the bags anyway, on his way out, but when he saw Parker in the doorway he gave that up and just ran. Parker jumped down to the asphalt and watched Liss dash across the parking area, bent low and weaving as he went. Parker stood where he was, shotgun in both hands, not pointing anywhere in particular.

Mackey leaped down beside him, empty hands closed into fists. "Shoot the cocksucker! What's the matter with you?"

"No need," Parker said. "And a noise could draw a crowd."

Furious, Mackey said, "Don't leave him *alive,* God damn it." He acted as though he wanted to pull the shotgun out of Parker's hands, and was restraining himself with difficulty.

Liss was out of sight now. The police had finished clearing out of here a little after ten, and the three in the trailer had gone to sleep around midnight, three hours ago, Liss on the sofa in the office, with the money and the guns. He could have just taken the money and left, but he hadn't wanted Parker and Mackey behind him the rest of his life.

Apparently, Mackey returned the feeling. "Parker," he said, "that was a mistake. We could have afforded a little noise, not to have him around any more."

Parker never saw any point in arguing over past events. He said, "Can you call Brenda?"

"Yeah, you're right," Mackey said. "We can't stay here any more." Peering away into the night where Liss had disappeared, he said, "He'll need time to get guns and friends, but I'll bet you, Parker, he still thinks this money is his."

8

Parker sat on the weedy ground, the chain link fence against his back, the reloaded shotgun on his lap. Out ahead of him, in the darkness, beyond the narrow strip of scrubland, the empty asphalt parking area stretched across to the big round bulk of the arena. Off to the right, its metal side picking up the glints of distant streetlights, waited the construction trailer. The three sacks of money were back inside it, and the padlock was once more in place on the door.

Parker had been seated here for twenty minutes, and so far nothing had happened. The only weapons they had were the shotguns, so Mackey had gone off unarmed to find a phone booth and call Brenda. She'd come to where he was, pick him up, and then drive on to the arena.

This town wasn't George Liss's home base, so he shouldn't immediately be able to lay his hands on guns and colleagues. There was time enough.

The car that nosed into the parking area entrance, way over by the arena building, wasn't a station wagon. It paused just inside the parking area, then switched off its headlights. In darkness, it drove slowly around on the asphalt, stopping two or three times, pausing, then driving on, moving in apparently random ways.

Liss? With friends? Parker lay flat against the fence, shotgun tucked in against his side, and watched the car move around the parking area like a hunting dog that's lost the scent.

Eventually the people in the car saw the construction trailer and drove over to it, still with no lights. They stopped beside the trailer and two men got out, one from the front seat and one from the back. When they opened the two right-hand doors, the interior light went on, and Parker could see that neither of them was Liss. Nor was the third man, the driver. The strangers shut the car doors, killing the light, and went over to look at the trailer, poking at its padlock.

Parker sat up, holding the shotgun in both hands. If they tried to break into the trailer he'd have to move against them. He had extra shells in his shirt pocket, but could only fire twice before having to reload. He should be closer, to put one charge into the two at the trailer door and the other into the driver. To give them something as a distraction while he reloaded.

Slowly, silently, he got to his feet and moved to his right, to put the bulk of the trailer between himself and the three newcomers. But as he edged up closer they moved away from the trailer, losing interest in it. Parker hunkered down, and the two guys got back into their car. In the brief moment when the interior light was on, he could see they were arguing among themselves, all three. He could hear the driver grind gears, and the car jerked away.

It made one more stop, over by the arena, and Parker saw the light come on briefly as the two guys got out again and went over to look at the accordion gates closed and locked over the broad arena entrance. They didn't seem to have anything particular in mind. They *were* dogs who'd lost a scent.

Finally they got back into their car, and this time it drove away entirely, out the exit from the parking area and out of sight. Two minutes later, another pair of headlights appeared way over there, and when Parker hunkered down next to the trailer to silhouette the car it was the station wagon.

This vehicle switched down to parking lights as it turned this way, then came straight across the empty lot to the trailer and stopped. Brenda was driving, Mackey beside her.

Mackey, more sensible than the strangers in the other car, had removed the bulb from the interior light, so nothing flashed when he climbed out and came across to Parker and said, "Did you make those guys?"

"Don't know them," Parker told him. He still held the shotgun and kept glancing toward the parking area entrance.

"Our delay is," Mackey said, "they were watching the motel. They followed Brenda when she left to pick me up. She took some time and shook them before she got to me, and told me about it, and damn if they weren't right ahead of us three blocks from here. We hung back and watched them come in and fuck around and then come back out. What did they do in here?"

"Looked lost," Parker said. Now he leaned the shotgun against the trailer and did the combination on the padlock as he said, "They know something, or they think something, but not enough. They came over here and sniffed around the trailer, but not as if they knew for sure this was it. It's like they think we didn't leave, but they don't know what happened instead. They were trying to figure out how to get into the arena, like maybe we're still in there."

"Friends of Liss?"

"Or Carmody's girl friend," Parker suggested. He pulled open the trailer door. "Too many people hanging around."

"Time to go someplace else," Mackey agreed. He opened the station wagon's cargo door, and he and Parker carried the three duffel bags from the trailer to lay them side by side on the station wagon's floor, like mail sacks. Then Parker put the shotgun in the office with the other two and plugged the bomb into the electric outlet beside the desk. He and Mackey got into the front seat with Brenda. They drove away from there, and three minutes later the trailer exploded itself into a million guitar picks.

9

Brenda drove, Mackey sat in the middle, and Parker was on the right. He bent his head sometimes to look at the outside mirror on his door, but nothing showed behind them. Four in the morning, this was a quiet town.

Except, of course, when a construction trailer blows up with a force that rattles windows a block away. The trio in the car heard it go, and Brenda immediately pulled into the curb among a line of parked cars, cutting the lights and engine. They kept their heads down and waited, and a couple minutes later the parade of official vehicles started: fire engines, police cars, emergency service trucks, all thundering along at top speed, sirens wailing and red-and-white gumdrops and tootsie rolls flashing.

The flow of excited public servants lasted five minutes or so, and finally ebbed with the appearance of a bright red fire chief's station wagon, making a slower and more dignified approach to the scene.

They let that last one go by, and then Brenda started up their own station wagon and took them farther away from the center of excitement. "Where next?" she said.

Mackey said, "Well, we can't go back to the motel, I know that much. Those extra guys, whoever they are, that's where they'll go, back where they were watching Brenda, stake it out, wait for us."

"I know," Parker said.

Brenda said, "I want to tell you, Ed, I'll be leaving a whole lot of cosmetics back in that room."

"We'll buy you a suitcase of the stuff," Mackey promised her, "out of Liss's share."

"Good."

"But the other problem is," Mackey went on, "we can't go to that empty house where we were gonna stash the goods, because naturally Liss knows about that place, and he just might show up there."

"Well, we can't drive around all night," Brenda said, taking a random right turn. "Some cop'll stop us just on general principles, and then he'll want to look at our laundry back there."

Mackey said, "The same thing would happen if we try to drive *out* of town. This is a very tense location right now. And if we go check into some other hotel somewhere at this hour in the night, we're still drawing too much of the wrong kind of attention."

"What we want now," Parker said, "is an all-night gas station."

Mackey frowned, leaning against Brenda to look at the gas gauge on the dashboard. "Why?"

Brenda, quicker than that, said, "I saw one out by the interstate."

Looking past Mackey's confused frown at Brenda, Parker said, "We'll get out a block before you reach the place. You go on in, you tell the guy you just got off the interstate because there's something knocking under the hood and you don't know what it is."

"The dumb broad in the car," Brenda said.

"That's right."

Mackey's frown turned to a smile. "He puts it on the rack," he said. "Inside."

Brenda said, "So I better tell him it's something with the brakes. Otherwise, we'll just stay outside by the pumps and he'll look under the hood."

Mackey beamed at Brenda's profile. "You see, Parker?" he said. "You see what I mean?"

"Yes," Parker said, and bent his head to look in

the outside mirror once more. Something? He squinted at the distorting mirror—*objects in mirror are closer than they appear* was etched into the glass—but there was nothing back there but parked cars, dark houses, streetlights, traffic lights playing solitaire. *Had* there been something? Hard to tell. Nothing now. Maybe it had been a car crossing an intersection back there.

It was another ten minute drive to the gas station, during which one police patrol car passed, going the other way. It slowed as they came together, the two cops giving the people in the station wagon a *very* long stare, but Brenda smiled and waved at them, and they nodded with dignity and drove on.

"One thing I don't want to have to do," Brenda said, sounding a little nervous as she watched the police car recede in her mirror, "is outrun a lot of cops in *their* town."

"At that point," Parker told her, "we give the whole thing up. Lose the car *and* the goods, and go to ground."

"Don't even think it," Mackey said.

They saw no more traffic, and then there was the gas station with all its gleaming lights, out ahead of them, an oasis of glitter in the surrounding dark. Beyond the station's lights, occasional smaller lights could be seen going by, fifteen or twenty feet up in the air; the big trucks on the interstate overpass.

"We'll get out here," Parker said to Brenda, "and we'll give you five minutes."

"Fine."

Brenda pulled the station wagon to the curb, and the men got out. Looking back the way they'd come, Parker frowned. Had something moved back there? As Brenda drove away, Parker stepped into the street, peering down the long empty stretch of it. No movement. Just the darkness.

"What is it?"

"Nothing," Parker said.

The gas station was on this side, a block and a half away. They crossed the street and walked down the opposite sidewalk. Facing the gas station was a closed tire store, with *sale* signs in the windows. They paused there to look across the way, through the large open doorway into the service area. Over there, Brenda was just backing the station wagon into the service area, on the side with the lift, being directed by a skinny kid in white company coveralls and his own baseball cap. He seemed to be the only one on duty tonight.

"We have time," Parker said. "I want a look at the ramp."

They walked on another long block to the two

on-ramps for the interstate, and saw a state highway patrol car parked on each one, tucked up partway along the ramp, so you'd already have made the turn before you saw it. "Just like we thought," Mackey said.

"Just like we *knew*," Parker said.

The one advantage was, where the highway patrolmen were, they wouldn't be aware of anything going on at the gas station. Leaving them there, keeping to the shadows, Parker and Mackey walked back and went beyond the gas station again before crossing to its side of the street and making their approach.

The kid had the station wagon up on the lift now and was checking the brake fluid, which should have kept him occupied, except that there was a bell over the office door that sounded when Parker entered, Mackey coming in behind him. Parker went to the doorway connecting the office with the service area, while Mackey went straight to the messy metal desk and riffled through the drawers, shoving credit card slips and other junk out of the way.

The kid came in fast, polite and ready to serve, but holding the wrench he'd used to open the brake drum cap. "Sorry, gentlemen, I didn't hear your car come—" He took in the absence of a car out by the pumps at the same time he saw Mackey at the desk. "Hey!"

Mackey straightened, shaking his head at the kid, disappointed in him. "You don't have a gun in here," he complained.

Bewildered, the kid stared at Mackey and said, "No! What do we want with a—? What are you *doing* there!"

Mackey came around the desk toward the kid, spreading his empty hands, saying, "That's a hell of a thing. What if we were robbers?"

It had crossed the kid's mind that that's just what they were. Blinking from Parker to Mackey, both of them now too close to him, he said, "You're not?"

"Not at the moment," Mackey said, and grinned.

Parker held out his hand. "If you give me the wrench," he said, "the lady behind you won't have to crack your head open."

Everything was happening too fast; the kid could never get set, never get a response ready before the encounter took another turn. Looking over his shoulder, he saw Brenda there behind him, holding up a shiny large socket wrench for him to see. She wasn't smiling. She looked businesslike. The kid said, "You're *with* these guys?"

Mackey laughed. "She's the boss!" he announced. "That's Ma Barker!"

"The wrench," Parker said.

The kid shrugged, and handed it over. "If you're not gonna hold the place up," he said, "then I don't get it."

"We're all going to stay here a while," Parker told him. "Where do you turn off the lights?"

This astonished the kid more than anything so far: "You want to *close?*"

"You're getting a vacation," Mackey explained. "An unexpected brief vacation."

Parker tapped the kid's chest with the wrench, leaving a grease smear on the white coveralls. "The lights."

The kid blinked, then pointed at the circuit breaker box on the back wall behind the desk. "We do it there," he said. "You can't turn them *all* off, though. There's some stuff we've got to leave on."

"For now," Parker said, "just turn off the outside lights."

Reluctant but obedient, the kid did as he was told, wide-eyed, as though it were some kind of sacrilege to close a 24-hour gas station.

Next, they had him lower the hydraulic lift, to bring the station wagon back down, and shut and lock the service area door, a double-width overhead garage door full of rectangular windows. Then they looked around at their new environment and found, at the right rear of the service area, a door to a storage room that was tucked in behind the office. Long and narrow, the storage room was full of fan belts and cans of oil and high wooden racks of tires. The door was open, but there was a padlock on the hasp on the outside.

Mackey said, "Write down the combination, will you?"

"I'm not sure I know it," the kid said, deciding to be crafty.

Mackey shrugged. "That's up to you," he said. "We're gonna lock you in there now, so you won't be in our hair. I figured to let you out when we go, but you want to take your chances on somebody coming along, that's up to you."

The kid remembered the combination then, and wrote it on a service order pad. He also asked if he could bring into the room with him the two magazines from the desk that he'd been reading, and they said okay. He went in without trouble, dragging along a wooden chair and carrying his magazines. He even grinned at them tentatively as they closed the door.

Fixing the padlock, Mackey said, "Not a bad kid. A bright future, I think."

"A smart kid," Parker said. "He knows he wants a future."

They turned off the rest of the lights, shutting the station entirely. A little illumination seeped out from under the storage room door, where the kid was reading his magazines, but not enough to be seen out in the street.

Mackey and Brenda caught up on some of their missed sleep in the station wagon. Parker made himself as comfortable as he could on the vinyl stuffed chair in the office, feet up on the desk. He dozed off a few times, never for very long, and then one time he opened his eyes and it was daylight; six or six-thirty in the morning.

And what had awakened him was a city police car out there, just pulling to a stop, this side of the pumps. There was only one cop in it. He got out on this side, and turned his back to look out over the top of his car at the street, looking left and right. His uniform was the wrong size, legs too short, jacket too loose.

Parker put his feet on the floor and leaned forward. The cop turned and started toward the office, right hand unhooking the flap on his holster, closing around the service revolver in there. Under the police cap, it was George Liss.

TWO

1

Seven hours before some atheistic sons of bitches robbed the Reverend William Archibald of four hundred thousand dollars, he woke up alone in bed. "*Now* where the hell is she?" he said.

Tina, having heard the familiar rich baritone voice, immediately popped out of the bathroom, saying, "Here I am, Will." Her heavy ash-blonde hair framed that willing face in a mad tangle, still mussed from sleep. She was naked, and remained the only woman in Archibald's experience to overflow her birthday suit. "Is there something you want, honey?" she asked.

He looked at her standing there, open, amiable, those round cheeks bracketing a full-lipped mouth succulent with sleep. "Come to think of it," he said, "there is."

Fifteen minutes later, Archibald was whistling in the shower while Tina ordered breakfast from room service. By the time he was dressed in his pinstripe blue suit, white shirt and figured blue tie, his sleek jowls gleaming with aftershave and his pewter hair brushed into corniche waves, breakfast was waiting in the living room of the suite, set up at the table by the big window overlooking the view, which Archibald ignored. Every town was the same, finally, if you didn't live in it; just a collection of tall and short buildings containing people who might be helped by Reverend Archibald's ministry, and might help the reverend in return. Now, seating himself before his bacon and eggs, home fries, orange juice, toast and coffee, he said a heartfelt, "Thank *you*, Lord," and tucked in.

Tina appeared ten minutes later, having completed her daily transformation. In her pale gray suit, white blouse with neck ruffle and low-heel black shoes, with her hair tamed into a bun, her pale and subtle makeup, and her horn-rim spectacles—she was blind as a bat, and wore those glasses everywhere except in bed, where she got along quite well by feel—she was no longer the compliant and indulgent Tina of their nighttime hours, but Christine Mackenzie, conductor of the Reverend Archibald's Angel Choir. The mouth was still loose and carnal now, when she smiled hello, but when singing "Just a Closer Walk with Jesus" those lips could appear to be swollen with nothing more than heavenly love. Heavenly.

At Tina's place, across the table from Archibald, the breakfast consisted of half a grapefruit, two slices of dry toast and tea without milk. Tina was a lush girl inside that gray suit, but it was a lushness that could spill into over-ripeness, as they both well knew. Limiting herself to a diet that the monks of the Middle Ages would have chosen for penitent reasons, to the castigation of the body and the greater glory of God, but doing so for rather different reasons of her own, Tina managed to hold her abundance in check, to keep herself at a level that was no more than what the kikes call *zaftig*. (The bastards even have their own language.)

From the very beginning of his ministry, William Archibald had understood that *the appearance of propriety* was the name of the game. It wasn't merely that the appearance of propriety was as good as propriety itself, but that it was much better. If the appearance of propriety were steadfastly maintained—religiously maintained, you might say—a reasonably careful man could have it all; the rich rewards of religion *and* the rich rewards of life. And that's what he wanted: it all.

Archibald wasn't a hypocrite. He believed that man was a sinful creature and he said so, publicly and often, never excepting himself. He believed that his ministry had held back many a fellow human being from committing crimes and sins untold. He believed that his contributions to the social order, his civilizing influence on men and women who were in many ways still one small step from the apes, were practical and immense, and he *firmly* believed he was worth every penny he made out of it. His ministry had rescued drunkards, saved marriages, reformed petty thieves, struggled successfully at times against the scourge of drugs, cured workplace absenteeism and given a center and a weight and a sense of belonging to unnumbered empty, drifting, useless chowderheads. If, in his leisure moments, he liked to ball a big-titted woman, so what?

They were finishing breakfast when Dwayne Thorsen came in, looking brisk and competent in a gray suit that managed to be as respectable as Archibald's without competing with it. Dwayne's twenty years in the Marine Corps had left him lean and mean, and his seven years as Archibald's executive assistant had done nothing to change him. He still preferred his old cropped-short Marine haircut (the stubby hair pepper-and-salt gray now), his comfortable but ugly black oxford shoes, and his government-issue wire frame round-lens glasses, through which his pale eyes skeptically gleamed like the coldest sunny day in Norway, from which his thinlipped hard-working farmer forebears had emigrated a century ago.

"Morning, Dwayne," Archibald said. "Order yourself some coffee."

"Ate."

There was a third chair at the table, facing the view. Like the other two, it was armless, with a cushioned seat and delicately scrolled wooden back. When Dwayne's big-knuckled hand reached for it, the chair seemed to flinch, as though sure it would be kindling in a minute, but Dwayne merely pulled it out from the table, sat in it, ignored the view as much as the others had, ignored Tina as well—he usually did, facing her when he absolutely had to with a fastidious sneer—and said, "All set."

"Well, naturally." Archibald smiled at his assistant. "If you're in charge, Dwayne, it's all set."

Dwayne shrugged that off. "Morning news says six hundred of them camped at the arena last night."

Not unexpected. Since Archibald's crusades offered no advance sales and had no reserved seating or credit card sales or anything else except cash on the barrelhead as the customer walked in the gate, and since his draw had only increased with the television ministry, it was usual these last few years for a number of people to bring sleeping bags or deck chairs and camp out the night before at the gate of the stadium or arena where he was to appear, to be certain of getting in. Still, six hundred was a pretty impressive number, and Archibald couldn't help a little smile of satisfaction as he said, "Radio news or television news?"

"Both. Local insert on *Today,* and just about every local radio news spot."

Good. Archibald would have no trouble selling out this twenty-thousand-seat arena, but it was nice anyway to let *other* people, people who so far were insufficiently aware of the Reverend William Archibald, know that this attraction was such a grabber it drew six hundred overnight campers. Better than the World Series.

Dwayne went on, "Security's shitty at this place, though I don't suppose it matters."

"Dwayne," Archibald said comfortably, sopping up the last of his egg yolk with the last of Tina's second piece of toast, "you say that every place we go."

"It's true every place we go," Dwayne said. "These outfits today, they're not used to cash."

"Dwayne, Dwayne," Archibald said, "who's going to steal from the ministry?"

"Well, we've had some, now and then."

"Pilfering. Employees, misguided smalltime people. You find them out, Dawyne, you always do, and I give them a good talking-to."

"And then I," Dwayne said, "kick their butts into the street."

"But we haven't had anybody like that for a long time," Archibald said. "You pick those people with a great deal of care, Dwayne."

"Which brings me," Dwayne said, "to this boy Carmody."

Archibald sighed. "A knottier problem than most," he admitted.

"I think we ought to get rid of him."

"For zealousness? Dwayne, we've never had to do anything like that before, and I just worry it could backfire on us."

"He's making trouble," Dwayne insisted. "He's an infection that could spread. I like my troops motivated."

"Yes, of course. But the press, Dwayne. The press is a constant affliction. If Tom Carmody's disaffection led him to the wrong reporter, if he found a sympathetic ear in the media to listen when he says we threw him out because he *got religion,* it could be very bad. Very bad."

"Three days' wonder."

"Maybe. And maybe it's open season on servants of the Lord right now, Dwayne, and we ought to, as our corporate friends say, protect our asses."

"I don't like what he says to the troops," Dwayne insisted.

Archibald understood what Dwayne's problem was. The Marine Corps method of dealing with rotten apples was to seek them out, identify them, and throw them away before they could infect the rest of the bushel. But the Marine Corps didn't have to worry about the combination of a naturally hostile press and a business dependent on voluntary contributions. What Tom Carmody could do to sow doubt in the minds of Dwayne's troops was *nothing* to what he could conceivably do, with the right reporter's help, to sow doubt in the minds of people like the six hundred drinking their thermos coffee at the moment out at the arena. Employees come and go, but the six hundred are needed forever.

Which it would not be politic to explain to Dwayne, an essentially simple soul whose range of comprehension was unlikely ever to extend beyond the perimeter of the brigade. If someone was troublesome to Dwayne's troops, that's all he would see or care to see; the larger picture was beyond him.

Archibald said, "I tell you what. After the crusade today, I'll have a chat with Tom, see if I can bring him round a bit."

"Fine," Dwayne said. "But, Will, *look* at him when you talk to him. Look him over. Keep an open mind. If he isn't gonna come around, tell me. I won't just fire him, I'll ease him out, so he don't get mad."

The idea of Dwayne being tactful brought a faint smile to Archibald's lips. He said, "I'll study him like the lesson of the day. How's that?"

Tina said, "Maybe you could talk him into joining some monks or something. Go into a monastery. Then he'd be away from us, but he'd be happy."

Dwayne always squinted a bit and looked away when Tina spoke, as though a bright light were being shined on him. He did that again now, and left it to Archibald to say, "Tina, that's a very good idea. I'll sound him out. A monastery is an *excellent* place for a religious young man."

"He's got a girl friend," Dwayne said, with no inflection.

Archibald raised an eyebrow. "*Has* he? So much for the monastery. Is she part of the problem, do you think?"

"Probably. Don't know for sure."

"Perhaps I should talk to them both together."

"She isn't here," Dwayne said. "She isn't one of us. She lives back in Memphis," he explained,

Memphis being Archibald's home base, where he had his Eternal Jesus Chapel and where his television ministry was taped.

"Well, I don't think we should postpone the issue until we get back to Memphis," Archibald said. "I'll talk to Tom this afternoon, after the crusade, and if necessary, talk to the girl later, when we get home. What kind of girl is she?"

"Don't know," Dwayne said, and shrugged. "Mary something. Don't know a thing about her."

2

Just around the time William Archibald was whistling in the shower, Mary Quindero was beginning to die. She knew it, or suspected it, or feared it, but couldn't warn her murderers because they refused to hear anything except the answers to their questions, and she had no more answers. They, Woody Kellman and Zack Flynn, didn't know she was dying because they had no idea of the cumulative effect of the strangle-and-reprieve, drown-and-reprieve methods they were using to get the answers they felt she was still holding back. And her brother, Ralph Quindero, couldn't know what was happening because he was over at Zack's place, watching an old horror movie on the VCR, unable to be present while his friends pressured his sister, and not realizing just how stupid they were.

"Don't hurt her, or— You know, don't do— She's my sister, you know, I gotta . . ."

"Don't worry, Ralph, when she sees we're serious, what's she gonna do? What's her choice? We gotta pressure her a little, that's all, so she knows we're serious. That's all."

That it hadn't worked that way was simply a miscalculation on everybody's part, starting with Ralph, who hadn't believed his pals would actually harm his own sister, and continuing with Woody and Zack, whose knowledge of the world came from movies and TV, which hadn't told them that, in real life, you could kill a person by repeatedly holding her head underwater in a bathtub, and finishing with Mary herself, who was motivated by a foolish desire to protect her dumb younger brother and who couldn't believe until too late that he wouldn't at some point come in and make them stop. But he didn't.

No. Ralph watched the horror movie until the finish, then brooded at the telephone while the tape rewound, wondering if he should call Mary's place, just see what was going on. This was taking longer than they'd expected, wasn't it? An hour and a half. What could take an hour and a half? How much information could Mary have, after all, and how long before Woody and Zack got it out of her?

Without the movie to distract his thoughts, he found himself worrying a little more about his sister in the hands of those two guys. They wouldn't . . . fuck her or anything, would they? No, they wouldn't do that, because they knew she'd tell him about it afterward, and they knew he'd *kill* them if they went too far, if they even— if they did anything except what they'd already agreed on: Lean on her a little, get whatever else it was Tom Carmody had told her about the guys who were out to grab the preacher's money, then phone him here to go downstairs and wait at the curb.

When Woody realized her eyes were open underwater, and that some new kind of sullen limpness had come over her body, different from the times when she'd passed out, he had an instant of panic, quickly buried. Ignoring the knowledge he already possessed, he pulled her back up out of the tub and stretched her out once again on the white-tile bathroom floor. Her eyes stayed open, water drops standing on them, not at all like tears.

"Passed out again," Zack said, disgusted, looking over Woody's looming back, his view obstructed.

Woody felt a sensation he hadn't known for

years, had completely forgotten: Being a little
kid on a swing, going too high, until his balls felt
like they were being sucked downward right out
of him, drawn into the frozen middle of the
earth. It had been a scary, exciting, unpleasant
but fascinating feeling then; now it only made
him sick. "Aw, shit, Zack," he said, and moved to
the side, a strong and heavyset but clumsy guy, to
let the skinnier tenser Zack have a clear view.

When the tape rewound, Ralph popped it out
of the machine and into its box, and considered
the rest of Zack's tape library. The three of
them, punks in their mid-twenties, inseparable
schmucks since high school, were occasional
burglars, and Zack loved to break into video
rental stores, copping armful after armful of
tapes while Ralph and Woody searched the cash
register and drawers for chickenfeed.

"How can we *call* him? Jesus Christ, Zack, his
sister's *dead!*"

"*He* doesn't know that. He doesn't know that
till long after we got the money, till we're gone
and *history*, man."

"*Jesus*, Zack."

"Call him, goddamit. You wanna run *with*
money, or without?"

Ralph touched the rows of tapes. Was it too
early in the day for porn? Nah; he selected a
tape, and turned toward the VCR as the phone

rang. And now he was almost reluctant to answer.

In the living room of Mary's apartment, the bedroom and bathroom doors both closed, Woody stood holding the phone, while Zack glared at him. They were both sopping wet, and hiding their fear from one another. "Remember!" Zack hissed. "She's locked in the closet! She's okay!"

Woody nodded impatiently and said into the phone, "Ralph? Okay, everything's done here. She's fine, we locked her in the closet, you can let her out when we get back."

Zack stared, wild-eyed, a ventriloquist no longer sure he controls his dummy. Woody said, "Well, she didn't want to tell us for a while."

Zack looked alert, worried, imperiled. Woody said, "You know, she always wanted to keep you out of—wants to keep you out of trouble. You know how she is."

Zack silently pounded the sofa back in frustration, and Woody said, "Well, she seen we weren't gonna take no for an answer, that's all, so then she opened up. She didn't know much more than she already told you, by the way. Not as much as we figured."

Zack nodded in exasperated agreement—so much effort, such a rotten accident, for so little return—and Woody said, "Except the name of the motel where Carmody's supposed to get in touch with them, if anything changes. Yeah, where they're gonna be today. So that was worth it, huh?"

"I don't know," Ralph said, hefting the porn tape in his other hand, thinking about how mad Mary was going to be, even when he came back successful, even when he had more money than *God* in his hands and all her irritating little doubts and sermons and putdowns were proved for once and all to be wrong, wrong, wrong. "I guess so," Ralph said. "Okay, I'll see you downstairs."

It was a five-hour drive from Memphis to where William Archibald's crusade had latterly taken him; they should get going, if they wanted to be there in time for the robbery. "Ten minutes," Ralph said into the phone. "Right."

He watched five minutes of the porn movie, rewound it, and went downstairs.

3

Lunch for the staff on crusade days was simple and short; bowls of salad, slices of bread, plastic cups of tea or apple juice, all laid out on long folding tables in whatever arena they found themselves. It's true this was an inexpensive way to feed a crowd, but Archibald's motives went beyond the squeezing of a dollar. He wanted his angels, his choir, his assistants, all his boys and girls to be cheerful and energetic and sparkling during the crusade to come, not bogged down by great sandwiches of cheese and meat, dulled by rich desserts, logy with milk shakes. And the staff enjoyed it, too, enjoyed the camaraderie of paper bowls and plastic forks, the rough fellowship of bleacher seats while eating and big open barrels for their trash afterward, the sense of coming together in peak condition to face the long and arduous campaign ahead: the saving of souls.

Dwayne Thorsen always ate like that anyway. He didn't see how people could stuff their faces with all that bad crap available to the idiots of this world. He'd eaten sparingly as a child back in Kentucky, out of necessity—they were *poor*— had turned necessity into virtue, and now virtue had become mere habit. But a good habit.

Among the first to start lunch, and the absolute first to finish, Dwayne discarded his implements in the empty trash barrel and began a roving tour of the facility, a kind of stubborn prowl, movement mostly for its own sake, to relieve the pressure he felt, the weight of responsibility on his shoulders. The rest of them could laugh and joke together down there in the bleachers, take it easy, pay no attention to their surroundings, and if something screwed up they'd just shrug and go on about their business. Because avoiding the screw-ups *was not their business*. Not even Archibald's business, not really. The smooth functioning, the seamless progress, the glitch-free continuation of the William Archibald Crusade; that was Dwayne's business.

This is what he'd learned in the Marines: Do not ask why, only ask how. That's the philosophy he'd carried out of the Marines and into his work with Archibald, and it's what made him so valuable. Irreplaceable. Whether Archibald were sincere or a phony, or some mingling of the two, wasn't Dwayne's concern. His only concern was that the crusade go forward with no bad publicity, no awkward snags, no loss of money, no distractions from the task at hand. None.

His roving of the stadium showed the security weak spots, showed the crowd-control difficulties, but showed also the advantages of the terrain, the narrow-funneled egresses, the vast clear space at the center of the stadium that meant no troublemaker could get very close to Archibald during the crusade without being seen and intercepted.

Dwayne visited the money room—fairly well concealed, fairly well protected—he visited the temporarily erected cubicles where counseling would be available at the end of the crusade, he visited the sexually segregated changing areas where the choir and angels would soon be getting into uniform (he didn't think in terms of 'costumes' but 'uniforms'), he visited the public restrooms and the refreshment area, he personally tried every door that was supposed to be locked and opened every door that was supposed to be unlocked.

Half an hour before the gates were to be flung wide to the paying public, Dwayne noticed from high in the stands Tom Carmody making his way across the Astroturfed field toward the dressing rooms, and even from way up here something about the man's posture snagged his attention. When something within Dwayne's area of responsibility was *wrong*, out of alignment, not exactly where or how it should be, he'd always spot it right away, and in this moment he could see that something about Tom Carmody was well and truly bent out of shape. The discouraged slope of those shoulders, the defensive clench of that ass, the fatalistic half-grip of those dangling hands as he made his way across the great open space; if they'd been back in the Marines together, Dwayne would know those signals could only mean one thing. A fellow bent on desertion.

But desertion? Here? If that were it, if Tom Carmody were merely planning to quit this livelihood and take his miserable long face somewhere else, Dwayne Thorsen would do nothing but cheer him on his way. Help him pack. But Tom wasn't leaving, not willingly, Dwayne was sure of that much. And here, in William Archibald's crusade, what would be the equivalent of desertion?

Dwayne followed Carmody into the dressing rooms, and came upon him hanging up his angel robe on a hook on the wall of the small and simple doorless cubicle he'd been assigned. His makeup tubes were already laid out on the narrow white Formica shelf in front of the mirror. His jacket was tossed on the floor in the corner; another bad sign. Dwayne said, "How you doing, Tom?"

Carmody jumped, guilt all over his face and in his every move. Guilt about what? Had the son of a bitch *already* found his reporter? Was he in here wired? Was he walking around with camera and tape recorder to expose the villainy of the William Archibald crusade? Dwayne considered, for just an instant, having Carmody searched, right here, right now, but realized at once and reluctantly what a mistake that would be if it turned out he'd jumped the gun, if Carmody were still merely gearing up for his betrayal, whatever form that betrayal would take.

The son of a bitch can't even look me in the eye, Dwayne thought, as Carmody said, "Oh, hi, Dwayne," and busied himself with an unnecessarily long search in his canvas tote bag for his clothesbrush.

Dwayne stood in the cubicle doorway and watched Carmody brush the robe, too hard and too long. Unconsciously echoing the counselors who would be at work in nearby cubicles in just a few hours, he said, "Anything you want to talk about, Tom?"

"What? *No,* Dwayne, everything's fine!"

Scared eyes, weak mouth, defensive hunch of shoulders. Oh, you'll bear watching, my lad, Dwayne thought. "Well, if you get troubled about anything, Tom," he said, doing his damnedest to put some warmth into his voice and failing even more than he knew, "I want you to think of me as somebody you can count on, somebody you can trust. A friend." He choked on the word, but got it out pretty smoothly, all in all.

A panicky smile played like summer lightning over Carmody's ashen sweating face. "I appreciate that, Dwayne," he said. "Thank you for— Thank you for worrying about me."

"Oh, I worry about everybody," Dwayne told him, with his own ghastly smile. "You know me."

"I sure do, Dwayne," Carmody said.

Dwayne nodded, and turned away. I wish I could send the son of a bitch on night patrol, he thought, and shoot him.

4

Zack sat behind the wheel of the maroon Honda Accord, Woody beside him, Ralph in back. In the parking lot at the Seven Oaks Professional Building—three law firms, three dentists, one interior decorator, one office for rent—diagonally across from the Midway Motel, they remained in the positions they'd held since they'd driven away from Memphis. There was nothing to do now but wait.

Ralph leaned his forearms on top of the front seat, so he could be part of the conversation. If you could call it a conversation; Zack said almost nothing, and Woody kept babbling on and on about nothing at all, as though silence were something to be feared, like a fatal disease. As he babbled, they all kept looking at the station wagon parked across the way at the motel, in front of room 16. The woman and one of the men were in that room, George Liss and the other man next door. They were tough-looking, all of them, even the woman.

Mary had pointed out George Liss to Ralph a couple of weeks ago, as the crook her friend Tom Carmody was mixed up with, that she was so worried about. (So worried, in fact, that she'd made the mistake of talking it over with her stupid kid brother.) The hardness of Liss's face had been daunting, but nevertheless, the instant he'd heard Mary's story Ralph had known what he had to do. And while he and Woody weren't real tough guys, Zack was, wasn't he? Zack could front for them in the toughness department. And Ralph, the way he saw it, was the brains.

Nothing happened for a long time, except that Woody just kept on talking, never saying anything at all interesting but never letting up. After a while, Ralph took his forearms off the seat and sat back to relax, not needing to follow every word. And when he looked out the left rear window, he could still see that station wagon over there, just as well.

The chatter was getting to Zack, too. He started saying things like, "You already told us that, Woody. Shut up." Or, "Who gives a fuck, Woody?" Finally, he turned around in exasperation and said to Ralph, "Remember that pizza place? Back a couple blocks."

"Yeah?"

"Go get us something. Maybe if we put a lotta food in this asshole's mouth he'll shut up a while."

Woody said, "I'm just filling the time, Zack. Jeez, what's wrong with just—"

"Shut your *face*."

Ralph said, "What if they go before I come back?" Gesturing at the station wagon across the street.

"They won't," Zack said, and looked at his watch. "It's an hour before the fucking crusade even starts. They won't go before the money's in."

"Boy, am I gonna spend *that* money," Woody said, grinning like Bozo the clown at the two of them. "I dunno, do I get a Jap bike, or a Harley?"

Woody had already thrown this question out to general consideration twice before. Zack leveled a furious glare at Ralph: *"Go."*

"Okay, okay," Ralph said, and got out of the car.

Zack watched in the rearview mirror as Ralph went sloping away in the sunlight, goofing along like some stumblebum on his way to the soup line. Woody continued to yak away. When Ralph passed out of sight, Zack took the spring knife out of his pants pocket, opened the four-inch blade, turned sideways, and slipped the knife point past Woody's arm and into his side, maybe a quarter-inch deep, just above the lowest rib.

Stunned, scared, Woody recoiled against the door to his right, and Zack pursued him, pressing the blade against his flesh, maintaining that slight and dangerous penetration, his expression grim and intent.

"Jesus, Zack! Jesus! What are you doing?"

Quiet, but very serious, Zack said, "If Ralph tumbles, what happened to his sister, I'm putting this in there to the hilt."

"What'd I say? Jeez, all I—"

"You been too jumpy," Zack told him, holding the knife in place. "Too jumpy just for what we're doing here. You're running off like an idiot. When Ralph comes back, you shut up."

"Come *on*, Zack—"

Zack pressed the knifepoint into Woody's side just a little deeper. "Wake *up*, you fucking asshole."

"*Don't*, man! That hurts!"

In the rearview mirror, Ralph was coming, a six-pack of soda on top of a pizza box. So soon. Zack frowned at the mirror, then at Woody. "You will shut up now, asshole, or I start cutting. You got me?" He gave the knife a quarter turn.

"*Aaaaa!* That hurts!"

"*And,* he figures out what happened back home, you're dead meat. You got it, Woody?"

"Yes!"

Walking back toward the parking lot in the sunlight, carrying the pizza box in front of himself in both hands like a page boy carrying the queen mother's crown, Ralph saw Zack leaning way over to talk at Woody, and from the menacing shape of Zack's posture Ralph knew Woody was being told to *shut up.* Scaring the shit out of him, Ralph thought, and grinned at the idea. Yeah, Zack would be their tough guy, against those other people.

As Ralph opened the right rear door of the Honda, Zack moved leftward, wiping both sides of the knife blade against Woody's thigh, leaving a small faint streak of bloodstain. Woody, grimacing in pain, put his right hand over the wound like a compress and pressed it there with his left elbow. Zack, in better humor, said, "So what'd you get? Pepperoni?"

"They could do halfies," Ralph told him, sliding into the car, pushing the box ahead of himself across the seat. "Half plain, half pepperoni."

Zack held up the knife, showing it. "I got my knife out, to slice."

"The guy did it at the place. Eight slices."

"I'll just leave it here," Zack said, putting the

open knife on top of the dashboard, "in case we need it."

Woody looked at the knife open on the dashboard, and blinked, and didn't say a word.

They ate the pizza, and drank three cans of the soda, and then across the way the doors of 16 and 17 opened, and the four people came out. The woman got behind the wheel of the station wagon. Two of the men were carrying duffel bags that they put in back, then all got into the car.

"She's the driver," Ralph said, surprised. "I didn't think she'd be part of it."

"Some women are," Zack said. "Why not."

"I'll have to tell Mary when I get back," Ralph said. "How good things could go, if you had a woman along you could trust to be on your side, and not be nagging you and putting you down all the time."

Woody put his right fist up to his mouth and gnawed gently on the knuckles. His left arm was pressed to his side. He wasn't talking, he was just staring at the glove compartment door. His left side ached, as though he'd been hit there by a baseball bat or something, not the sharper pain he would have expected from being stabbed. I've been stabbed, he thought, with dulled surprise. How did I get to be here, in this place, stabbed? Jesus, what did I do that I'm here in this place?

COMEBACK

Zack started the Honda engine, and they followed the station wagon, keeping well back, and it did what they'd expected it to do, it went straight to the stadium. There, the wagon stopped, and the three men got out. They collected their duffel bags and strode away across the full parking lot, and the station wagon moved on, and Zack followed.

Back to the motel. The woman went indoors, and Zack found their old parking spot beside the Seven Oaks Professional Building still waiting for them. "This is nice," he said, as he pulled to a stop in the same old space. "They pull the job, and if it works out she goes and picks them up, and gets them out safe, away from the law. And then we go in and take it away."

Nobody said anything. Zack gave Woody a hard smile. "Pretty good, huh, Woody?"

I don't want to be here, Woody thought. I don't want to know these people any more, or be in this place, or anything. I don't even want that pizza, it feels like shit in my stomach, I don't know if I'm gonna throw up or cry.

He didn't do either. Zack reached out with his middle finger and tapped the bloodstain on Woody's thigh and repeated his question: "Pretty good, huh?"

"Yes," Woody said.

5

During football games, this was the replay booth, where guys with video equipment could second-guess the referees. It wasn't an ideal command post for Dwayne, being so far from the center of activity, but its overview of the stadium couldn't be beat, and the communications between here and the rest of the complex were perfect. Dwayne, not a sitting-down type, paced back and forth behind the long plywood table containing all the electronic equipment, and looked out past it through the line of big windows at the crusade making its measured practiced way far below.

The main part of the crusade, exclusive of counseling and other activities scheduled for afterward, was planned to take just two and a half

hours, and the second hour was not quite over
when the phone call came. There were four telephones spaced along the plywood table, and the
low-pitched ring was supplemented by a white
light that blinked on the appropriate one.
Dwayne picked it up, said, "Thorsen," and heard
a frightened young male voice say a scrambled
nervous sentence in which one word stood out.

"Robbed."

Dwayne made it to the money room before
the police, but not by much. The normally
locked door was propped open, and inside Tom
Carmody lay unconscious on a sofa, his gray-
white angel makeup blotched with dark dried
blood. Dwayne looked at that unconscious dis-
contented face and knew: "So this is what you
did, you stupid fuck," he said, and turned as the
first cops came in.

In every organization, there's the one guy who
manages things. Not the boss but someone at
the middle level, the equivalent of a master
sergeant in the army. Dwayne was that one in
William Archibald's Christian Crusade, and
whenever he had to deal with another organization of whatever kind he always sought out his
opposite number, and would settle for nothing
less. This time, it was a fellow named Calavecci, a
Detective Second Grade.

Tom Carmody had been ambulanced away still unconscious, the six people in the money room had been questioned and turned over to the medics for tranquilizing, and now the money room had filled up with technicians. Dwayne stood to one side, observing, waiting, and when he heard a voice say, "Who's in charge of security here?" he smiled and turned around, knowing the manager-type on the other side would be just as anxious to make contact with *him.*

"Me," he said, and felt an instant coolness toward the man filling the doorway. Large but not beefy, with an irritable yet patiently amused expression, he was the kind of guy, in the Marines, who liked war too much. Well, you worked with who you had. "Dwayne Thorsen," and he approached with hand stuck out.

The man considered him briefly, considered his hand, then took it. "Calavecci, Detective Second Grade. What happened here?"

"Three men with shotguns."

"Inside help?"

"Yes."

Calavecci looked surprised: "Usually we get denials," he said, "this early on."

"This isn't early," Dwayne said. "They're already gone with the money. I don't have time for denials."

"Good. Got a candidate for the inside guy?"

"Tom Carmody. The one went to the hospital with a concussion."

Calavecci considered that. "Trouble before?"

"He's been building," Dwayne said. "I had my eye on him. I expected something different, though."

Calavecci looked around the room. "They whomped him to give him cover," he said. "Whomped him pretty good, but that was it."

"That's right."

"Be nice," Calavecci said, "if he knows where they went, because *we* sure as hell don't."

Dwayne didn't like that. "You mean they're long gone?"

"I mean they're pros," Calavecci said. "Like you and me. So they're on the next page already. Maybe the loot's in the trunk of a car outside and they're back in here with the audience. Congregation? What do you call this crowd?"

"The crowd."

"Well, maybe they're with them. Or maybe they're burning rubber on the interstate, but if they are we've got them, and I assume they know that, so I assume they're not. So maybe they come to town last month and rented a little apartment two three blocks from here. We're checking that. We'll check everything. But it would be nice if your fella, whatsisname—"

"Tom Carmody."

"Be nice if he knew what was supposed to happen next," Calavecci concluded. "Take all the guesswork out of it, that's what *I* like."

Carmody was conscious when Dwayne and Calavecci got to the hospital, but the doctors wouldn't let him be questioned. "Bullshit," Calavecci said, which was the wrong thing to say to the doctors.

"Hold on," Dwayne said. "Let me try something."

"Try anything," Calavecci offered, "just so your friend can tell us where *his* friends got off to."

So, while Calavecci went to ask the Memphis police to question Mary Quindero, just in case Tom had told the woman anything useful, Dwayne called the hotel, and Archibald was there in the suite all right, raging in the background when Tina answered the phone in that breathless lisp that made Dwayne's skin crawl. Listen to the man back there, yelling his way around the hotel suite; how he hates to lose money. "Let me talk to Will," Dwayne said.

"Oh, *Dwayne,* he's *so* upset, I know he wants to talk to you."

He did. Dwayne stood there at the pay phone in the hospital corridor and listened to a certain amount of unnecessary oratory and then at last cut in with, "Will, you can help down here."

That caused a stumble in the oration. Archibald said, "Help? Down where?"

"I'm at the hospital with Tom Carmody. They won't let the law question him, so it's up to you and me. They can't very well keep the man's religious advisers away from him, so *we* do the questions."

"Questions? Tom?" Dwayne could almost hear the penny drop. "Dwayne! Do you really think that filthy little pervert— You think it's *him?*"

"He's part of it. Come on down, Will."

In a small bare conference room borrowed from the hospital administration, Dwayne gave Archibald a little orientation talk before they went in to see Tom: "Now, listen, Will. If we get mad, or we make him scared, we won't get a thing out of him."

"I'd like to get his liver and lights out of him, that wretched little . . ." Archibald sputtered, at a loss for words he could permit himself to use.

"Will, that's the wrong attitude," Dwayne said patiently. "What we want is whatever information Tom Carmody has inside his head, and the *only* way we're gonna get it is if we go in there and preach sweet forgiveness."

"Sweet for—!" Archibald choked on the word,

his beefy neck flushing all the way around his collar.

"Shit, Will, you play it to millions all the time. This once, play it to one. We want the money back, dammit."

"Yes, we do," Archibald agreed, and sat back, and nodded. "All right, let me just get myself settled."

"Sure."

Archibald sat there a minute longer, eyes half closed, and when he made a steeple of his hands Dwayne thought in astonishment that the man was going to pray, but he didn't. He took a deep breath instead, managed a smile, got to his feet, and said, "All right, Dwayne. Let us go pour oil on the little prick."

6

Miserable, hurt, alone, knowing at last what an utter fool he was, Tom Carmody lay on his back in the high hard bed in this small bare-walled one-patient hospital room and tried to decide what to do. Suicide; confession; silence followed by a life of atonement; silence followed by revenge on—

On whom? Revenge on whom? Which brought him full circle to suicide once more. Who else should he be avenged on, except himself?

Mary. Would they think Mary had anything to do with the robbery? Just because they were friends? Because he'd told her about— That he would *never* let them know! Never bring her name into it at all, never, never.

His head was heavily bandaged, all across the

top and around the back, the thick white layers covering his ears and even pressing his eyebrows down lower over his eyes. He lay cocooned, sounds muffling as they made their way through the swaths of cotton. Why had Grant hit him so hard? Why hit him at all?

Of course, this way at least the police would never suspect, would have no reason to believe the person brutally attacked by the robbers was himself a part of the scheme. So, if he *didn't* confess—

He kept remembering Grant, on that first meeting, look at him with his cold eyes and say, "If the police catch you, they won't ask your motive." No, they won't.

But he could ask his own motive. Had he ever expected to get away with it, or had he unconsciously been trying to get himself caught all along? Had he ever realistically expected to collect his half of the take? When he didn't even know where they were going with the money from here, where to find them afterward? He knew George Liss's name; the others had probably used aliases. If George wanted to go on pretending to be an honest citizen, if he actually showed up next month at the parole office, Tom could make contact that way. What were the chances?

And what did it matter? An IV tube fed something or other into a vein in his left forearm; surely, if he wanted to kill himself, he could use that needle somehow. He might even be able to get to his feet and go out that window over there.

Wait, he told himself, trying to keep control of his mind, fighting the panic, the guilt, the fear. Wait. Wait to see what happens.

And then Archibald himself came in, followed by Dwayne Thorsen. Tom looked at that smug fat face—he barely registered Thorsen's colder harder face behind the preacher—and his resolve hardened. I'll admit nothing, he promised himself. Nothing.

There was one chair in the room, armless with tubular chrome legs and green vinyl seat and back, and of course Archibald immediately took that for himself, pulling it over to the right side of the bed and sitting where he could comfortably peer into Tom's face, his own face a mask of false sympathy. Naturally it was false, Tom knew better than to trust any emotional display from William Archibald. His skepticism, however, did not yet lead him to believe that Archibald's falseness was anything beyond the normal insincerity that defined the man's life. He did not at all guess that this time the fakery covered an absolute certainty in Tom's guilt.

"How *are* you, Tom?" Unctuous, oily, the moist eyes melting with sympathy. Meanwhile, his hatchet man, Dwayne, leaned his forearms on the footrail of the bed, watched Tom like a specimen in the zoo, and made no attempt at all to show anything other than his normal cold indifference.

"Not feeling so good," Tom said, and was surprised to hear the quaver in his voice. He didn't have to pretend weakness, did he? Weakness and confusion. No pretense at all.

"Guess that fella hit you pretty hard," Archibald said, and nodded in faux sympathy, agreeing with himself.

"Yes, sir."

"Shows you what can happen with those bad companions," Archibald said, face and voice as smoothly caring as ever.

Tom didn't absorb the meaning of the words for the first few seconds, and then a sudden jolt of icy cold ran along his spine, as though a great icicle had all at once formed there. His lips trembled. Tears filled his eyes, but didn't fall. "S-s-s-sir?"

"What I think happened, Tom," Archibald said, gazing into Tom's eyes as though Tom were the greatest TV camera ever made, "I think we all just got caught up in the money too much. You, and me, and Dwayne here, and all of us."

"I don't know what you mean," Tom said. He tried to keep his own face expressionless, but couldn't help staring at Archibald like a bird in front of a snake.

Archibald ignored Tom's feeble protest. With a theatrical sigh, he said, "I don't excuse any of us, Tom, no, I don't. We've all been culpable in this matter. I should have spent more of my time talking about what the money *does,* not just how we have to go out and get more of it."

He's a liar, Tom reminded himself, he's a liar and a charlatan, and he's just trying his usual crap on me, that's all it is. Tom *knew* that's all it was, and he was right, and he knew he was right, and yet he found himself being tugged in nonetheless, drawn by that syrupy voice and those smooth words. Grasping at inessentials because he didn't dare think about the essentials, he said, "The money doesn't do any *good.*"

"Oh, but it does, Tom," Archibald said, "and that's where I've been remiss. Remiss, Tom. I've failed you, and I've failed the Crusade, and I've failed every good soul who has ever put his or her trust in me. Because all I've been saying is, 'Give me money,' and I have *slighted,* I have *ignored,* I have failed to make clear, what the money is for."

"It's for you," Tom said, feeling amazingly brave to confront the man like this, to throw the truth in his face for once, with no softening of the blow at all.

"It's for the Crusade," Archibald corrected him, but gently, the milk of human kindness still sheening on his face. "The television costs us *so* much, Tom, but without the television how will we reach God's creatures? And the counseling, the crusades in the field, all our efforts . . . Now, I know some of the good we do is strictly speaking not in His service, is more social work than religious work, but I believe God can and will forgive us for our lunch programs and our school crusades and—"

"The money's for *you!*" Tom cried, feeling himself sink under Archibald's platitudes, drown in his false pieties, lose his own hard certainties in the undifferentiated sludge of Archibald's philosophy. "It's all for you! The rest of it, it's all just fake, it's all just to cover for you, for you, for you!"

Archibald sighed, more sinned against than sinning. He sat back in the small chair, gazing with sad forgiveness at Tom as he contemplated what had just been said, and finally he replied, "I had suspected that was what you believed of our mission, Tom. I'm glad you've unburdened yourself of it, brought it out in the open where we can look at it."

"It's true, and you know it."

Another sigh. Archibald said, "And I suppose that's why you helped those men."

A hard wall. There, right there, in the path of Tom's life. A huge hard impenetrable wall, right there *now*. His throat pained him, his eyes pained him, with the emotional sense of his loss. He looked at the stolid Dwayne Thorsen, then back at Archibald. They were waiting for an answer. And he too was waiting to hear his answer. He and they all wanted to know: Would Tom lie? At this point in his life, at this nexus, at this nadir, would he lie? or would he tell the truth?

"Yes," Tom said.

Archibald's long sigh this time seemed more honest, more human, and even Dwayne shifted position slightly, though his face didn't alter. Archibald, as though the question hardly mattered, said, "And do you know where they are now, Tom?"

"No."

"Oh, Tom," Archibald said. "Don't disappoint me at this stage, Tom. You have started to open your heart, don't close it again."

"I don't know where they are," Tom insisted. "And that's the truth."

Archibald and Dwayne shared a glance. Tom knew they were trying to decide whether or not it *was* the truth, and he knew Archibald didn't really and truly care whether Tom believed all that stuff about the money, all that face-saving garbage about lunch programs and counseling and of course his own work with former convicts. *There's* a laugh; the work with former convicts. How do you like your social programs now, Reverend Archibald?

Archibald turned his attention back to Tom. "I hope to do what I can to help you," he said, "in your difficulties with the law. And I equally hope *you* will—"

A knock at the door interrupted him. Archibald frowned at Dwayne, the unctuous mask slipping slightly, and Dwayne silently crossed to the door, opened it, spoke briefly in a low voice with someone outside, accepted a sheet of paper, and shut the door again.

While Archibald and Tom watched, Dwayne came back to the bed, reading the sheet of paper, which was white but flimsy, curling at the edges. Archibald, tension at last apparent in his voice, said, "Dwayne? What is it? Do they have the rascals?"

"No," Dwayne said, and extended the sheet of paper for Archibald to take. The paper curled like parchment as it changed hands, so that for one instant there was something almost Biblical in the transaction.

Archibald unrolled the paper, read it, and the blood drained from his face. *That* expression of shock wasn't false. Tom stared at the soft clean hands holding the sheet of paper; he burned with both fear and curiosity, wondering if they would even tell him what the paper was all about. And then Archibald looked at him with something new and incomprehensible in his eyes. Sympathy? The genuine article?

Extending the rolled-up sheet of paper, Archibald said, "You should see this, Tom. And I am truly sorry."

What in God's name could it be? Fear clenched Tom's chest as he took the paper and fumblingly unrolled it. A fax, on the letterhead of the Memphis police. It was addressed to Detective Second Grade Lewis Calavecci, and the body of the message read:

"Mary Quindero discovered dead in her apartment. Preliminary medical exam suggests death by drowning. Body found in a closet. Under the circumstances, we'd appreciate more particulars regarding your interest in this person. Please forward your response to—"

"NO!"

"I'm sorry," Archibald said, and this time he sounded as though he really meant it. "Do you have any idea why they would do such a thing?"

"No." Tom gestured vaguely with both hands, too distracted to think. "No! They didn't have to— They didn't even *know* about her until . . . I didn't think they knew about . . . There's no *reason*."

Softly, almost whispered, Archibald said, "Who are they, Tom?"

Tom let the paper go, and it curled into a tube on the blanket covering his legs. "The first one," he said, in a dead dulled voice, "is called George Liss. I met him in the parole program . . ."

Around midnight, one of the night nurses foiled Tom's suicide attempt. He'd been trying to slit his wrists with the IV needle torn from his forearm. The tool was inefficient, making a number of shallow gashes, painful and disfiguring but not in any way fatal.

A doctor from emergency was called, who oversaw the cleaning and bandaging of the wounds. Tom spent the rest of the night strapped into the bed, horribly awake, thinking unwillingly about Mary and the people who had killed her. Why? *Why?*

George Liss. Let them find him, please, God. Let them find George Liss.

7

When George Liss ran across the dark parking lot away from the construction trailer, he expected a bullet in his back at any second. He had no idea what had gone wrong, why Parker and Mackey weren't dead right now and he on his way with the four hundred thousand, but Liss was not a man to gnaw at the past. All he would do now was run, as fast as he could, bent low to make a smaller target but nevertheless expecting that bullet every step.

Which didn't come. He hadn't run directly toward the lights flanking the entrance, not wanting to silhouette himself, but had angled off toward the darkness along the perimeter fence, and when he reached that fence with neither a bullet in his body nor even the sound of shots

having been fired behind him, he began to believe he might be still alive. And with work to do.

Hunched over, Liss trotted along the straight
chain-link fence, and slowed when he got near
the brighter illumination around the entrance.
Looking all around as he moved, he decided
there was no one there, no one watching, nothing to worry about, at least not in this particular
spot at this particular moment, so he sprinted on
through and out to the public road.

And now what? He still wanted the money,
that was the whole purpose, but Parker and
Mackey were alerted now, would be harder to
deal with. And right this minute, this town was a
dangerous place to be wandering around in,
alone and unarmed and with no good explanation for his presence. There were going to be
cops all over the neighborhood tonight. Somehow he had to go to ground, get out of sight.

What were the choices? He couldn't get to the
motel and Brenda and the station wagon before
Mackey called to warn her what had happened.
And if he went to the empty house where they'd
planned to stash the goods once they'd left the
construction trailer, Parker and Mackey were
sure to show up eventually, cautious and armed.

But if he just hid out in some alley or parked
car for the night, Parker and Mackey could clear
out entirely, find some other place to wait for the

heat to grow less intense, and Liss would never get his hands on that money. There had to be a way to stay out of sight, and yet keep an eye on those golden duffel bags.

Across the road from the stadium parking lot was a row of old three-story houses, with small shops downstairs and apartments above. Shoe repair, deli, dry cleaners, all shut down solid for the night, with heavy gates closed over their windows and doors. The apartment windows were all dark, too. Was there something useful there?

A nearly full trash barrel stood by the curb. Out of it Liss plucked a newspaper. Folded in quarters, he put it under his left arm, and now he was a nightworker on the way home.

Headlights coming. Liss turned and strode purposefully the other way, not too fast, not trying to conceal himself. Two cars went by, civilians, and then one in the other direction. At the corner, Liss crossed the street away from the stadium, and when he walked past the side of the final row house he saw that it had a back yard, all those houses had back yards, separated here from the sidewalk by an eight-foot-high wooden fence, vertical boards tapering to points at the top.

With a door? Yes; a simple narrow door of the same vertical boards, probably nailed to horizontal support pieces on the inside, and with a little round metal Yale-type lock inset in the wood. No knob.

Liss looked left and right, and saw no one. Dropping the newspaper onto the sidewalk, he lifted his right knee high, and slammed his heel flat against that lock. The door popped open with one loud *crack*. Liss stepped through, pushed the door closed again behind himself, leaned against it, and looked around at where he was. Illumination from the streetlight on the corner showed him a messy untended yard, scattered with junk. A shorter wooden fence of the same style but only about five feet high defined the other border. An exterior flight of metal stairs against the rear of the building led up to a second-story door. The back door of the ground-floor shop was under the stairs.

Liss made his way through the junk across the yard to the other fence, and looked down the row of yards. Some were neater than this, some as messy. A few had been turned into cared-for gardens and some had outdoor furniture in little conversational groups. Almost all the yards were defined or separated by some kind of fence. Every house had the exterior metal staircase giving access to the second floor. Every window down the entire block was dark, and the outside darkness was deeper the farther you went toward the middle of the block.

COMEBACK

Liss went over four fences, looking for the yard with the least sign of activity; neither a garden nor an accumulation of junk. He wanted a yard that suggested either a vacant apartment or a stay-at-home tenant, and when he found the right one he went silently up the stairs to that second-floor door, and just as silently through the door with a credit card.

He was in a kitchen, small and old-fashioned, not remodeled for maybe thirty years. There was very little light, just enough to suggest the place was neat, cared for. He opened the small old refrigerator with its rounded corners and found it contained small amounts of just a few things; milk, orange juice, a few eggs, some tiny leftovers in plastic. A solitary; good.

The refrigerator's interior light, in the few seconds he'd had the door open, had spoiled his night vision. He stood patiently in the middle of the room, one hand touching the refrigerator door, until shapes took form in his sight again, and then he moved forward, through the deeper darkness of the doorway on the other side of the room.

Night vision no longer helped. Shuffling forward very slowly, as silent as possible, both hands moving to the sides and out ahead, Liss made his way down a short black hall with a pair of closed doors facing one another partway along. A little farther, his groping right foot touched the saddle of a doorway. He stopped. He felt the wood of the frame, then the closed door itself, and then the old faceted glass knob. He turned the knob as slowly and gently as though it were a safe in the back of a store still open for business, and when it gave a tiny *chick* sound he eased the door open, out away from himself.

Light, thin diffuse gray light defining the rectangles of two windows. This was the small living room, facing the street. Liss came on through, still holding the doorknob turned, and reached his other hand around to grasp the knob on the other side. He held that one in the same position as he eased the door shut again, then turned to look the place over.

A living room, underfurnished. Two sagging armchairs, one near each window. A small TV, on a low wooden crate. A couple of end tables and lamps. One side wall was absolutely empty; that's where the sofa would have been.

Liss crossed the room and looked out a front window, just in time to see a car turning in at the parking lot entrance across the way. Brenda? No, it wasn't the station wagon. Liss sat on the arm of the chair behind him, and watched through narrowed eyes. Who was in that car? What did they want?

The car made its hesitant moves around the

parking lot, and Liss tensed up when it stopped over by the construction trailer. People out of the car, fucking around over there at the trailer. He didn't like that, he didn't want anybody else around his money. That's my money, he thought. Keep away.

"Who's there?"

Liss automatically rose to his feet, while his mind registered that voice. Old, male, querulous. Liss moved catlike away from the windows.

"Who's there? *I* hear you!"

Liss slid along the empty wall, coming the long way around to the door, so he'd wind up behind it when it opened.

"You better speak up! I've got a gun!"

Oh, have you, Liss thought. Good; I need a gun.

The doorknob rattled. "I'm warning you! I'm coming in!"

Do it and get it over with, Liss thought.

The door opened. Liss leaned close to it, eyes fixed on the gray rectangle of window past the dark vertical line of the edge of the door. A figure moved into that space, and Liss clubbed down with his forearm, hitting the top of a shoulder, the side of a neck. The old voice cried out, and Liss swung around the door, punching hard into the indistinct figure, connecting three times before it could fall.

Light switch. Should be beside the doorway, same side as the knob. Yes; Liss flipped it, and a ceiling light came on, the bulb discreetly behind a round pink glass saucer.

The unmoving old man on the floor bled slightly from nose and mouth. He wore gray pajamas and a thick wool maroon robe and dark blue slippers. Liss rolled him over, frisked him, searched the floor all around him, and there was no gun. The old son of a bitch lied.

Liss switched off the light, hurried back to the window, and was just in time to see that unwelcome car come across the parking lot, moving as slowly and hesitantly as ever, and jounce out the exit onto the street. It drove away, out of sight.

Good, Liss thought. I don't know who you people are, but stay out of the way.

8

Zack was still driving. He steered them out of the stadium parking lot and down the empty street, as Ralph said. "All for nothing, the whole thing for nothing."

"We don't give up," Zack said. He'd grown less cocky, but more sullen and just as determined, since he'd lost the woman in the station wagon.

When she'd come out of the motel, moving with purposeful speed, all three of them in the car had perked up, even Woody, who'd been sulking about something for hours. And at first they'd liked it that she was pushing hard, driving a little too fast for the city streets. It meant action at last, something happening.

They'd heard on the car radio about the half-million-dollar robbery—a half a million dollars!—and they knew the robbers had gotten away with it clean and clear. They were still at large. And this woman in the station wagon would lead them right to it.

Except she didn't. "Shit," Zack said at one point, "she's onto us."

"Oh, goddamn it," Woody said. "I knew it'd be something." His brief return of high spirits was over, already.

Ralph was leaning forward again, forearms atop the front seat. "Maybe she isn't," he said. "What makes you think she is?"

"We went down this block before," Zack said, angry and disgusted, "and made that *fucking turn!*"

Half a block ahead, the woman took a right turn very hard and fast, the heavy body of the wagon sagging way leftward as she went around the corner and out of sight. Zack took the turn as fast as he could, not quite as quick as the woman, and when they came around— God-damit, the station wagon's coming the other way!

How did she *do* that? A hard right, an impossibly tight U-turn to the left, and coming back the other way as Zack completed his own turn. All three of them gaped at her, and she pretended they weren't even there. A good-looking woman, dramatic in the rose-glow of her dashboard, jaw set, eyes facing front as she flashed on by.

Ralph twisted around to look out the back window, and saw her take a left so fast and so sharp she left rubber all over the street back there. Going back the way they'd come. And of course, by the time Zack got them turned around and back to the intersection she was long gone.

Still, he drove in her imagined wake for a while, as they argued about what it meant and what to do next. "It doesn't come out right," Woody kept saying. "Everything screws up, it just gets worse and worse, we should never of got into this, we're fuckups, that's all, we're just fuckups."

"Shut up." Zack's knuckles were white, he held so hard to the steering wheel. His teeth were clenched, the veins stood out on the side of his neck, he looked like he'd explode. But he never shouted. "Shut up shut up shut up." Low, quiet, but with such intensity that Woody withdrew down into a sullen lump in his corner of the front seat.

Ralph said, "Shit, Zack, we did lose her. I mean, we *lost* her."

"So we'll *find* her."

"How?"

"The stadium. That's where she was headed, before she saw us. So that's where we'll go."

And that's where they went, and got nothing for it. Nobody at the stadium, all locked up and dark. Parking lot empty except for some construction trailer way at the far end, padlocked and empty. Nobody and nothing. No trail of breadcrumbs. With no alternative, they drove away from the stadium at last, the car moving along in its own gray cloud of depression.

"What we did," Woody mumbled, feeling so sorry for himself he was almost in tears. "What we did, and for nothing."

"Shut *up*, Woody."

"What we did, what we did."

Ralph frowned at Woody's miserably unhappy profile. "What are you talking about?"

"He's talking about," Zack snarled, "what an asshole he is. It isn't over, all right? We aren't done, all right?"

Ralph said, "Zack, we don't know where they are. If the cops can't find them, how are *we* gonna find them?"

"Luggage," Zack said.

Woody was still deep in his own misery, but Ralph bit: "Luggage?"

"She didn't take any luggage when she left the motel," Zack said. "None of them did. Just those duffel bags, and that was for the job. Remember, the radio said. So they didn't take their luggage, so they're going back."

Ralph felt a sudden surge of hope, and even Woody looked up. Ralph said, "To the motel!"

"They're going back," Zack said, absolutely sure of himself. "And so are we."

Same parking space. The nearby pizza place was closed, but they found another and settled down in their usual vantage point to eat and to wait. Across the way, the windows of rooms 16 and 17 were dark. No car parked in front. Not back yet.

After a while, Ralph said, "Maybe they're hiding the loot. Maybe they're doing that first, so it won't be on them if they get stopped."

"That's okay," Zack said.

"But maybe it won't be with them," Ralph said, because Zack didn't seem to be getting the point.

"That's all *right*," Zack said. "If it isn't with them, they'll tell us where it is. Okay?" Zack pulled that switchblade out of his pocket again, snapped it open, whapped it down onto the dashboard where he'd kept it before. "With *that*, okay? We'll ask with that, and they'll tell us."

Ralph looked at the knife, the blade glinting sharp, reflecting a nearby streetlight. Troubled by a sudden thought, he licked his lips and said, "Zack? That isn't how you asked Mary, is it?"

Woody made a small sound deep in his throat.

Loud, covering Woody, Zack said, "Of course not! Jesus, Ralph, we didn't cut her, all right? I never even showed her the knife. Jesus Christ."

"Okay," Ralph said. "Okay."

Zack gave Woody a disgusted warning look, then reached out to switch on the radio. "Let's hear something cheerful for once," he said.

They listened to Top 40s, interspersed with news reports. They kept hearing about the three robbers and the half million dollars and how the three robbers were still on the loose, and it never occurred to them. They sat there in the parking lot, visible to the street, three guys in a car with out-of-state plates, listening to the news reports about how every cop within five hundred miles was looking for the three robbers, and it never occurred to them for a second, not until about twelve million watts' worth of searchlights and floodlights were suddenly beamed at them from every direction in the universe, including a helicopter up above.

"Jesus!" Zack cried, blinded by all the light, and would have made the fatal mistake of switching on the car engine if Ralph hadn't been just smart enough to yell, "No!" and grab his elbow.

They sat in the car in the empty parking lot, impaled by all that light, specimen bugs on a display board, and shadows moved out there. Cops, armed to the teeth, easing through the light as through heavy fog, moving cautiously in this direction.

"You in the car!" A hugely amplified voice, coming from everywhere. *"Don't move! Make no movements!"*

Woody started to cry. "I don't fucking believe this," Zack said, but it wasn't clear whether it was the cops' sudden presence or Woody crying that he didn't believe.

Ralph, amazed at his own capacity for quick thinking, leaned another inch forward over the seat back and said, "We didn't break any laws. We're driving to the coast, we stopped here for a pizza and rest a while."

"Right right right," Zack said. He was blinking like mad, his fingers twitching on the steering wheel.

One cop, braver than the others, approached Zack's door, opened it, and stepped back. He was carrying a shotgun—a freaking *shotgun,* for Christ's sake!—at port arms, and what he said was ridiculous: "Sir, would you step out of the car, please?" *Sir!*

"Officer," Zack said, his voice sounding much younger and more vulnerable than usual, "officer, uh, something wrong, officer?"

"Just step out of the car, please, sir."

So Zack, fumbling a bit in nervousness, stepped out of the car, and the cop asked to see

ID, continuing with the horrible grotesque parody of politeness. In the car, Woody hunched down in his corner of the front seat, moaning, while Ralph kept unwillingly looking at that switchblade knife on the dashboard, as big as a bayonet in all that light.

Zack's driver's license was handed on back to some other cop, and then more cops approached the car, also loaded down with weapons, and called on Ralph and Woody to get out, which they did. Woody, no longer crying, just stood there and trembled, like a horse on the way to the dogfood factory, while Ralph looked all around, trying to see, interested despite himself in what was happening.

More *sirs*, more requests for ID, more licenses passed back into the darkness behind all that light. Then the frisk. *Sir*, would you face the car? *Sir*, would you place your hands on the car roof? *Sir*, would you move your feet back? Farther apart, *sir*. Thank you very much, *sir*.

Pat pat pat; nothing. They were permitted to stand normally again, feeling a little better. Damn good thing the two pistols were stashed with their bags in the trunk.

"Sir, would you mind opening the trunk?"

They stared at one another, stuck, screwed, completely fucked over, and another cop came out of the darkness into the light to say, "Which one is Quindero?"

A distraction from the question of the trunk. But was this a good thing, or a bad thing? "Me," Ralph said, raising his hand like a kid in school. "Ralph Quindero."

The cop was a little older than the other cops, and not in uniform, and with no guns in his hands. It was hard to see people's faces in all this light, expressions and features got washed out to nothing, but still Ralph had the feeling there wasn't much he'd like in that face. The plain-clothes cop, no inflection in his voice, said, "You're from Memphis?"

"Yes, sir."

"You know a Mary Quindero?"

Woody made the weirdest sound Ralph had ever heard, like a screen door being crushed or something. Ralph looked at him, just as Woody dropped to his knees, arms hanging at his sides. What the hell?

"Sir? You know a Mary Quindero?"

"She's my sister," Ralph said. "What's going on?"

The plainclothes cop turned away to the other cops. "Bring them in," he said, and walked away into the darkness, and Woody began to keen, like a dog when somebody's died.

9

Dwayne was in Archibald's suite, waiting. He didn't want to be there, but if he went to his own room down the hall Archibald would just keep telephoning every five minutes, so it was better to be here in the comfort of the man's suite, with Calavecci given this number to call if anything happened, even if that did mean he had to put up with Tina marching back and forth in a tight robe all the time, like a hooker on a runway, flashing those heavy legs.

Archibald marched, too, back and forth, back and forth, stopping every once in a while to glare at the phone, as though it had betrayed him in some fashion. "Why don't they *call?*"

"Cause they don't have anything to say," Dwayne suggested.

Tina, voice dripping sympathy, said, "Will? You want a massage? Come on in the bedroom, I'll give you a nice massage."

Well, Dwayne knew what *that* meant, but Archibald was too distracted by the loss of the money even to respond to his harlot. "No, I can't think," he said. "You go to bed, Tina, I'll be along later."

"I want to wait with you," she said, and so she did.

What was this like? In some ways, it was like a wake, sitting around being polite in the presence of a death in the family. More than that, it was almost as though the money hadn't been stolen, it had been kidnapped, and they were waiting to hear from the kidnappers, hear what the terms were for getting the money back.

When the phone finally did ring, at almost three in the morning, it seemed at first as though nobody was going to answer it. Archibald and Tina, both pacing, stopped to stare at the instrument, on a round table at one end of the sofa. Dwayne, seated at the other end of the same sofa, also looked at the phone, but didn't reach for it because this, after all, wasn't his suite. Then he realized that while he was deferring to Archibald, Archibald was deferring to him, as the professional in this situation. Once that became clear,

Dwayne lunged across the sofa, scooped up the receiver, and said, "Thorsen."

"Calavecci. You want to come down to Broad Street?" That was what they called police head-quarters, a big old pile of limestone built during the Wobbly scares, back in the twenties.

"You got them?"

"No, I don't," Calavecci said, "I'm sorry to say. I got something else, though. Very interesting."

"Be right there," Dwayne said, but of course he had to give Archibald about ten minutes of explanation about that one-minute phone call before he could leave.

Calavecci met him in a small barren office that had the look of a place whose regular occupant had just been fired, but which was in fact no-body's regular space. It was a meeting/confer-ence/interrogation room, with an extra chair in one corner for the stenographer, for when the confession was to be taken, and a phone on the desk for calling the stenographer.

Calavecci and Dwayne sat across the desk from one another, both comfortable in this room, and Calavecci said, "We couldn't believe we were so lucky, so of course we weren't. What we had was three white males in a car with Tennessee plates, where you people are from, and it's parked for hours in a professional building parking lot, where the building's closed for the night."

"Three's the right number," Dwayne agreed.

"But the wrong guys." Calavecci grinned and shrugged. "But interesting nonetheless. Your boy Tom Carmody—"

"The inside man."

"The clown," Calavecci agreed. "His girlfriend Mary Quindero turns up drowned in a closet. Not a usual way to go."

Dwayne, trying to be patient, said, "That's right."

"One of the three guys in the Tennessee car is her brother Ralph."

"Ah," Dwayne said, getting it. "Tom to George Liss to a couple of his pals, so that's our doers. Then Tom to Mary Quindero to her brother Ralph to *his* pals, they decide to do the doers."

"The sheer quantity of assholes in this world," Calavecci said, "never ceases to amaze me. You want some know-nothing clown come in, louse things up? No problem."

"But the sister's dead," Dwayne said. "How does that come into it?"

"The other two," Calavecci said, "Isaac Flynn and Robert Kellman—"

"Isaac Flynn?"

Calavecci shrugged. "That's what it says on his driver's license. Twenty, twenty-five years ago, people named their kids all kinds of stuff, like they were brands of cereal. Anyway, these two, Flynn and Kellman, they leaned on the sister because she clammed up when she realized what her brother had in mind. Of course, these are not guys who get the details right."

Dwayne shook his head, having trouble here. "They killed his sister, and the brother kept on with them?"

"He didn't know. He still doesn't know." Calavecci smiled like a wolf. "I thought you'd like to be here when we tell him, see what falls out of the tree."

He's tougher than I am, Dwayne told himself, a thought that didn't come to him often and which left him slightly uneasy. But if this was a test, he'd have no trouble passing: "Should be interesting," he said.

Ralph Quindero was about what Dwayne had expected: Beetle Bailey without the comedy, a sad sack who would always be in the wrong place at the wrong time. Just smart enough to get into trouble.

What do you do with such people? Dwayne had dealt with a number of them in his Marine years, and they were a real problem. They weren't mean or vicious, they were just inevitable losers who screwed themselves up and made trouble for everybody near them along the way.

Your only hope was a war; you'd put them on patrol till they didn't come back.

It was too late for a war to help Ralph Quindero, who came shuffling into the interrogation room with his guard and, at Calavecci's direction, sat in the chair Dwayne had vacated, Dwayne now being in the corner on the stenographer's chair, to observe. Quindero gave him one curious look on his way in, but Calavecci was clearly the authority figure here, and Quindero was doing what his brand of clown always did; once it's too late, be polite and cooperative with everybody. Ingratiating.

With Calavecci and Quindero seated facing one another, Dwayne in the corner, and the uniformed guard leaning against the door, Calavecci said, "Well, Ralph, you're a lucky man."

Quindero looked confused, as well he might: "I am?"

"Oh, absolutely," Calavecci said. "After all, what've we got on you? Eating a pizza in a parking lot. No crime there."

Quindero's slumped spine was beginning to straighten, hope was lifting him up. "That's right," he said, his voice tinged with awe.

"Of course," Calavecci went on, "there's the issue of those handguns in the trunk, but they weren't yours, right?"

"No, sir. They're not mine."

"And the car isn't yours. The car's Zack's, so the guns are *his* problem."

"Yes, sir!"

"Of course," Calavecci said, "if we wanted to get really technical . . ." He waited, and grinned at Quindero, a sly and nasty little grin.

Hope stumbled. Quindero began to fidget in the chair. "Sir? Technical?"

"Well," Calavecci said, "there's the matter of the robbery out at the stadium."

Quindero blinked, confused now. "Sir? I didn't have anything to do with that, we didn't, we didn't rob anybody!"

"But you knew it was going to happen," Calavecci pointed out. "That's why you came to town, because you knew the robbery was going to happen, and the problem is, you didn't inform *us* about it. You knew a felony was going to be committed, and you didn't inform the authorities, and that's called accessory before the fact. If we want to get technical, you know, just to be a pain in the ass with you."

Quindero didn't know exactly how to respond. He snuck another look in Dwayne's direction, then said to Calavecci, "The reason we came here? Sir, we were just—"

"Now, take it easy, Ralph," Calavecci said. "Be careful you don't say anything to make me think you're trying to be a smart guy."

"No, sir, no, sir, I'm cooperating."

"That's right. So's your pal Woody, by the way. That boy's singing like a miner's canary, on videotape. He's the one told us why you're here."

"Woody?" You could see Quindero trying to figure out where the bullet was coming from, so he could dodge it. Or try.

"Now, Tom Carmody," Calavecci said, "he was the inside man in the robbery, we know all that, Tom told us in the hospital. And Tom was good friends with your sister. Mary, is it?"

"My sister— Yeah, she's Mary. But she doesn't have anything to do with this!"

"Well, she did," Calavecci said. "Tom told Mary what was gonna go down here, and she told you, and so you and your pals thought you'd come on out, see what there might be in it for you. Isn't that right?"

"I, uh, I guess. But Mary isn't part of it!"

"Take it easy, Ralph," Calavecci advised. "The point is, you may have had something naughty in mind, but you didn't *do* anything yet. Unless, that is, like I said, we want to get technical with this accessory-before-the-fact business. But I don't think that's going to happen," he finished, and grinned at Quindero.

Who grinned back, falteringly, and said, "I'm glad. Thanks."

Calavecci nodded. "After all, we're gonna

want you as a witness, because the *other* two, you know, Woody and Zack, we got them on all kinds of stuff. The handguns, the accessory count, murder one—"

"What?"

"Oh, that's right," Calavecci said, snapping his fingers, "you don't know about that part. Still, your testimony's gonna be very important there."

"Nobody got killed!" Ralph's eyes were actually bulging, his breathing had become audible.

"You're wrong about that, Ralph," Calavecci said. "Somebody got killed, all right. Drowned in a bathtub. Took a long time at it, too, what I hear."

Panicky, Quindero leaned forward, hands gesturing out in front of himself as he said, "We didn't kill anybody! We just drove here, we parked, we didn't—"

"*Before* you drove here. Now, we could almost pull accessory on you there, too, but I accept it, you didn't know about the murder, so that's—"

"*What* murder? Nobody was murdered!"

"Oh, come on, Ralph," Calavecci said, grinning in high good humor, "figure it out. You can figure it out."

Quindero could, too, though he didn't want to. Watching the young fool's profile, Dwayne saw him struggle with it, shaking his head, half-saying words, taking them back, finally saying, as though it were all just nothing but a joke in bad taste, "No, come on." And then again, asking for mercy, decency, humanity, something, "No, come on, no."

"You know who it is," Calavecci told him, almost crooning now. "Spit it out, Ralph. Tell me the name."

Quindero's mouth hung open. His big eyes filled with tears. He couldn't seem to move or breathe or blink; certainly he couldn't talk. Calavecci studied him with mock sympathy, and then said, "Ralph? You really don't get it? Come on, boy, you're smarter than that."

Dwayne got to his feet, surprising everybody, breaking the moment. Ignoring the punk, he went over to the desk and nodded at Calavecci. "You're having too good a time," he said. "I'll be going off on my own now. That was the Seven Oaks Professional Building? Where you picked these people up?"

Calavecci didn't like being interrupted. Irritated, he said, "What do you mean, off on your own?"

Dwayne turned away, finished with Calavecci, and looked at Quindero's tear-stained face. "Shut up, kid," he said, "until you see a lawyer." And he left.

Sending them out on patrol was a lot cleaner.

10

When Bill Trowbridge woke up, he had to pee real bad. Also, he'd finished the magazines those crooks had let him bring into the locked storage room with him, when they'd taken over the service station. He'd slept for a while, curled up on the hard floor, but now he was awake, and he had to do something, soon.

He'd figured out who those people had to be. The news of the robbery at the stadium had been all over TV and radio yesterday afternoon, before he'd come to work. They'd said it was three men that had done the job, but they must have gotten that part wrong; it was two men and one woman. And they were hiding from the cops *here*.

What to do? They were tough and mean, no

question about that. They'd beat up one guy at the stadium so bad he was in the hospital. They were, like the radio and TV said, armed and dangerous. He was lucky all they'd done was lock him in here with the batteries and fan belts.

On the other hand, he did have to pee. And he didn't have any more magazines to distract his mind. And who knew how long they meant to keep him in here, or even if they'd remember to let him out before they left. Or if they even intended to let him out. So, for all those reasons, Bill Trowbridge was climbing the walls.

Literally. The room was deep and narrow, crowded with deep high wooden bins and shelves on both sides, all the way to the top, full of auto parts of various kinds. Fourteen feet up was the ceiling, obscured in darkness, far above the hanging light. Bill climbed up the shelves and bins, finding it easy, using the construction on both sides, and when he got to the top the ceiling was Sheetrock. He punched a hole in it with a length of tailpipe from one of the bins, yanked Sheetrock down and out of the way, dumping the pieces as quietly as possible into nearby empty bins—all the bins above the ten-foot level were empty, dusty, dry—and found two-by-six beams up there, sixteen inches apart. The roof, resting on those beams, was made of planks.

The storage room had plenty of tools. All Bill had to do was be careful about noise. Using screwdrivers, pliers, a flat-sided tire iron and a wrench, he gouged away sections of plank, exposing the tar paper and then the gravelly tar of the surface of the roof itself.

The more he worked, the easier it got, because the more room he had to work in. When he first broke through a section of tar paper and tar to the outer air, the sky was still black, but as he worked it began to lighten out there, and when he finally squeezed himself up between two of the support beams and out onto the rough-surfaced roof it was morning. Real early morning, but morning.

The first thing Bill did was go to the edge of the roof at the back of the building, where it overlooked a narrow stretch of scrubland with bushes and skinny little plane trees on it, and pee over the side, trying to hit branches that wouldn't make too much noise. Then he looked around, wondering how best to get himself down off this roof, and saw the police car!

Oh, boy; talk about luck. The police car was even coming *here*. Bill moved as quickly and silently as he could across the roof, seeing the cop get out of his car over there by the pumps and then walk this way, toward the building.

Standing at the front edge of the roof, just

above the office door, Bill waved his arms over his head to attract the cop's attention. "Hey!" he called.

The cop looked up.

11

The police were stretched thin, having so many places to search, so many routes to guard, so many barricades to man, so many possibilities to think about. That was why they were doing one-man patrols in what they considered the safest places, and how it was that Liss found a cop all alone in his patrol car, half asleep, parked next to a ramp for a narrow rusty iron bridge over old freight yards. There were a few bars and diners in this neighborhood, a few junkyards and machine shops and auto-repair places, but no homes, and no commercial places open at this hour. Liss circled around into the grassy steep slope above the freight yards, where an old chain-link fence was half broken-down, bent out of the way, rusted and useless. Along there, he found a two-foot length of the metal pipe that had originally been part of the frame of the fence, and held it close along his right leg as he came loping down the empty street toward the patrol car, clutching his upper right arm with his left hand as though he'd been wounded and yelling, "Help! Help!"

The cop, startled out of a moony doze, saw this wounded man running forward, scrambled rapidly and awkwardly out to the pavement, and took the metal pipe directly across the face. He fell backward, half in and half against his car, dazed but trying to reach his holstered pistol, and Liss slammed the open door into him, pinning him there while he swung the pipe three more times at that head.

When Liss pulled the door open, the cop slid to the ground. Liss quickly stripped the uniform off him, not wanting blood on it, and stuffed the body into the trunk, noting the shotguns on racks in there, the first-aid equipment, even a small red-handled ax. Couldn't be better.

The uniform fit fairly well; good enough. Sitting behind the wheel, engine and heater on, uniform cap on his head, police radio giving him the ebb and flow of movement through the night, Liss waited. No rush any more.

*   *   *

He'd had to rush earlier, hurrying out of the old man's house across from the stadium when Brenda showed up in the station wagon. As they'd loaded the duffel bags over there, Liss had looked around frantically for a car to steal, but there wasn't time, and in any case, with so little traffic at this hour, how could he follow them in a car without being spotted?

So he'd had to do it a different way. It was hard, there were times he thought he was going to fail, but he kept going. Out of necessity, he trailed them on foot.

What made it a little easier, they were driving slowly, carefully, obeying the law, calling no attention to themselves, stopping at every stop sign, waiting at every traffic light. They parked at the curb for quite a while when the construction trailer blew up and the streets filled with fire trucks and police cars and ambulances and all the rest of it, and he could take a breather then, hidden beside an exterior staircase to an old tenement building.

After that, when they moved he ran; when they stopped he walked. Sometimes their lights were just faint red dots far away, and once when they made a turn he thought he'd lost them completely. But he managed to keep up, and to see what their idea was at the gas station, and he admired the move. Indoors, safe, warm. They wouldn't leave till morning, and by then he'd be ready.

In the meantime, he dozed in the warm comfort of the police car, the crackly snarl of the radio's infrequent reports keeping him from the mistake of a deeper sleep, and at first light he got out of the car, stretched, went down the slope to relieve himself, got back into the police car, and drove over to the gas station to get rid of Parker and Mackey and Brenda and get, at last, the goddam money.

Would they be awake or asleep? It was still very early. They wouldn't expect trouble after so many peaceful hours hidden away. They didn't know anyone had any idea they were here. And what would they see when he first showed himself to them? A cop.

He parked at the gas pumps, like a regular customer, and walked toward the station building, getting the cop's handgun out of its holster. Advertising posters and grease-pencil announcements obscured much of the office windows, but as he came nearer he saw there was somebody in there, seated at the desk. Parker? Staring at him?

Did they still have the shotguns?

Liss was deciding to shoot through the plate glass, get it over with, when movement suddenly made him look up. There was something on the roof! Nothing but a silhouette against the gray morning sky, looming over him, a black figure like something out of horror stories, waving its arms and yelling. Without any thought at all, in quick panic, Liss raised the pistol and squeezed off a wild shot.

And then all hell broke loose.

THREE

1

Parker looked past the notices taped to the gas station window and watched Liss come this way across the blacktop, that handgun sliding out of the holster. Parker's hands splayed on the metal tabletop in front of him, and he looked down, remembering the shotguns, seeing only the wrench they'd taken away from the kid. He reached for it, even though it was useless, even though he knew Liss was smart enough to shoot him through the window, not bother to come inside. Why should he?

Parker picked up the wrench, and heard a shot. He stared out at Liss, almost a silhouette against the flat gray morning light out there, and the silhouette was arched backward, the arm

143

with the pistol aimed upward. Liss had fired at what? Something on the roof?

Parker heaved the wrench through the plate glass and launched himself out of the chair toward the open doorway to the service area. Would the racket wake Brenda? Would she know to get that station wagon moving?

The answer was yes, but she was even faster than Parker hoped. As he dove through the doorway, meaning to roll, to come up beside the wagon and yank open its rear door, the engine was already kicking over. Before he was on his feet, it was moving, and he came up to see the garage door splinter as the station wagon roared through it. Brenda hunched and grim over the wheel, Mackey just opening his eyes, his mouth a big astonished O, the car screamed through the wreckage it made of the door, spinning and sliding rightward over smashed plywood, bent metal, crushed glass.

Parker dropped to the concrete floor as the station wagon's rear wheels rifled broken pieces back into the garage, peppering the walls and tools with chunks of wood, metal and glass. He lay there, listening, hands and feet poised under him, trying to figure what was the best route now. What's the way out of this now?

A burglar alarm high on the front of the building began to scream, and Parker wriggled hurriedly backward, toward the office. If Liss came in here . . .

The doorway. He climbed it, trying to be invisible on both sides, and when he leaned leftward for a quick look out the office's smashed window he saw Liss running for the police car, the pistol waving in his hand.

Sure. Whether or not he knew Parker was still in here, and still alive, it was the money Liss wanted, the money he couldn't lose sight of.

Parker watched, because whichever way Liss went, that's where the money had gone. Liss jumped into the police car, kicked the engine on, spun the wheel, made a sharp U-turn around the pumps, and headed away to the left. Away from that interstate over there. Toward town.

Some ricocheted something had sliced Parker's left arm, not deep, but enough to sting. Rubbing it, he went out of the building through the opening where the garage door used to be, and above the insistent wail of the burglar alarm he heard a voice, some voice yelling. He looked around and saw nothing, but then remembered that Liss had fired upward, so he stepped farther from the building to look up, and the kid was up there, sitting on the roof. The kid they'd locked away in the storeroom was up on the roof, sitting there, both hands pressed to his left leg because that's where Liss had shot him.

He saw Parker down below, and yelled some more: "Help! Help!"

"Everybody needs help," Parker said, and turned away, and went loping toward town.

2

Parker walked two blocks. In the second, two police cars raced by him, shrieking, on their way to
the burgler alarm at the gas station. At the far
end of that block was a diner, just open for the
morning's business. Parker went in there, where
a dozen delivery men and salesmen yawned over
coffee in their separate spaces. He found a stool
at the counter with empty stools on both sides of
it, ordered breakfast, and in the mirror on the
back wall he watched the street behind him,
where an ambulance screamed past, toward the
gas station. The waitress brought his ham and
eggs and toast and coffee and the ambulance
screamed back the other way. Carrying the kid.

Parker ate, and looked at his own reflection in
the mirror, and except for the stained cut on his

left sleeve where he'd been nicked he looked all right. Like this is where he would eat breakfast.

Time to think. He knew the people. Did he know them well enough to find them?

Liss was the newcomer, but he was the easiest to peg. It was the dead side of his face that told the truth. A competitor, he'd never team up with anybody, not for long. If he had to go in with others to get what he wanted—like the money in those duffel bags—he'd take the absolute first chance that came along to get rid of his partners, and to get rid of them in a way that wouldn't leave anybody spreading complaints. Single-minded, he'd only look forward; never back. He wouldn't care if Parker was coming, because in his mind it would simply be somebody else trying for the same thing, the money. It wouldn't occur to him that for Parker that wasn't enough, that he wanted more than the money. That he needed Liss dead.

As for Mackey, he was a mechanic, like Parker. If Parker knew himself, he knew Mackey. He knew he wouldn't ever bother to cheat Mackey, because they were useful to each other and there'd always be enough for both of them. And he also knew he'd never go out of his way to give Mackey an assist, because Mackey was supposed to be a grown-up who could take care of himself. So that's the way Mackey would feel.

Which meant, at this point, Mackey would just keep moving, straight ahead. He wouldn't even consider the idea he could circle back and find Parker. Why should he? He couldn't even be sure Parker was still alive, back at the gas station. So Mackey would keep on, and Liss would keep on, right behind him, and if that's all there was to it, Parker would be the lame third, already out of sight and out of mind.

But that wasn't all. Brenda was also in the mix, and Brenda was the only one of them who thought about the future. She would want everything settled, now, today, before they all left this town. She would never want anything out of the past to come catch up with her, farther down the road. She was fast, and she was smart, and she was decisive—look how she tore that station wagon out of there—and Mackey deferred to her, because he'd learned long ago that when he followed Brenda's advice things worked out okay. So Brenda was the key.

Liss was following Mackey. Mackey would follow Brenda. Where would Brenda lead?

The station wagon was marked up now, it had to be. They couldn't keep it for long. Brenda would lose Liss, she was that good, but then she couldn't just drive around all day because very soon the cops would be on the lookout for the station wagon that had ripped through that garage door. And the kid would have already told them about the duffel bags in the station wagon, so the law would know it was the heisters from the stadium inside that car.

Brenda would lose Liss. They change cars, somewhere, somehow. Now there are three possibilities. They make a run for it, try to get out of town without being stopped by the law or Liss or anybody else. Or, the second choice, they hole up at the empty house where they'd all originally meant to wait out the police search. Or, third, they go back to the motel they'd been in before the heist.

If it was just Mackey, he'd choose to run. But Brenda's too smart and too careful. Does she go to the house? She knows Liss will be waiting for her someplace. And Liss will figure her to go to the house, right? Because that was the original plan for after the heist, and because, as far as Liss is concerned, the motel is used up. And Brenda will know that's what Liss is thinking.

What did Brenda say in the car, about the motel? "I'll be leaving a whole lot of cosmetics back in that room."

They'll have a different car. They already have a civilian cover in that motel. Brenda will believe that Liss will look for them in the house.

Parker paid for his breakfast, and left.

3

The Midway Motel occupied a wide shallow parcel of land on Western Avenue, across the street
from the Seven Oaks Professional Building. The
motel, red aluminum siding over concrete
block, with metal room doors painted to look
like wood, presented its long face to the street,
with blacktop across the front for guests' cars to
park, nose in. At seven-thirty that morning, cars
and pickups stood in front of eleven of the
twenty units, but not in front of either 16 or 17.

Parker walked down the other side of Western
Avenue and climbed the concrete steps to the
squat brick professional building. He stood in
the little lobby, looking at the directory, aware of
what was happening in the street. A few cars
went by; nothing else.

"Can I help you?"

It was a caretaker, looking nosy. Parker said, "No."

"Well . . ." The guy was miffed. "I'll be over here," he said, and went away.

Parker stepped outside and paused, like anybody, to study the weather and the day. Going to be sunny, not hot. Nobody moving around the motel. No cars yet this morning in the Professional Building's parking lot, no cars with occupants inside stopped up or down the street.

Parker still had the key to room 17 in his pocket. When no traffic was in sight, he crossed the street, moving directly to 17, watching for movement from inside any of those windows along the front, and there was nothing. Now the key and its rectangular plastic tab were in his palm.

He went in fast, slapping the door shut behind him as he crouched down and ran across the room, looking left and right. Nothing, nobody. In the bathroom, dark. Nothing, nobody.

The drape was already closed across the front window beside the door. Parker switched on lights and looked around, and nobody had been in here since they'd left except the maid. They all traveled light, all except Brenda and her cosmetics, and their goods, Parker's and Liss's, were still here where they'd been left, nothing but some clothing and toothbrushes and other things that didn't matter, weren't traceable, could always be bought new.

The original plan, now nothing but a memory, was that they'd wait in the construction trailer until the excitement was over. Then, at six in the morning, Brenda would pick them up, and they'd drive the three miles to the empty house, in town but isolated, and stash the money there. Then they'd come back here and stay in the motel until it seemed safe to leave town, when they'd go by the house once more, pick up the money, and be off.

Now everything was random. Mackey and Brenda and the money were somewhere in this city. Liss was somewhere else, looking for them. And Parker was counting on Brenda, sooner or later, wanting to come here.

There was a connecting door to the room where Brenda and Mackey had stayed. They hadn't bothered to unlock it before but Parker did now, and this room was also empty. And in this bathroom were Brenda's famous cosmetics, spread over every surface.

Parker switched off the lights in Brenda and Mackey's room, went back to his own, and closed the connecting door almost completely, leaving just a crack to see and hear through. Then he went into the bathroom in here, stripped off his shirt, and washed out the angry red line along his upper left arm. He found one last fresh shirt, put it on, moved a chair over near the connecting door, switched off the lights in this room, and sat down in the dark to wait.

Click.

Parker sat up straighter, and a vertical line of gray light appeared in front of him, brightened, darkened, went out.

Somebody'd come into Brenda and Mackey's room; that was daylight when the door had opened. It was no more than two hours, Parker thought, that he'd been waiting in here.

The lights didn't go on, in the next room. Parker leaned close to the door and heard very small movements.

Brenda and Mackey would switch the light on, right away. Was this Liss? Parker listened.

Now the lights did come on. And the sounds of movement stopped. Then there was brisk walking, past this door and beyond, and Parker heard the bathroom light click on. He eased the door open a bit more, but his angle of view was toward the front of the room. He could see most of the bed, on the opposite wall, and the bedside table, and the round table and two chairs and swag lamp in front of the window, and part of the window with its drape pulled across. He couldn't see the door.

More footsteps. The closet door was slid open. Ruffling sounds as somebody went through whatever clothes were in there. Then a drawer was opened, and shut.

Somebody searching. Somebody neat searching; he shuts the drawer. Knowing this wasn't Brenda, coming to believe it wasn't Liss, wondering if it was one of the three guys from that car that had nosed around the stadium parking lot, Parker waited, and then a guy he'd never seen in his life before came around the end of the bed and crossed over to look in the drawer of the bedside table.

Parker looked at this guy, trying to fit him in. A friend of Liss's? Was Liss waiting at the empty house, and he sent this other guy just in case the money showed up at the motel?

No. Liss wouldn't trust anybody else that far, and nobody else would trust him that far. Also, this guy didn't look the type. He was a very trim fifty, with short-cropped gray hair, wire frame eyeglasses, and a look of competence and self-assurance. He was dressed in a neat gray suit that made him look more like a cop than a banker, but this wasn't a cop.

Something like a cop? Somebody who doesn't mind breaking and entering, and who feels there might be something here he's looking for. Somebody who's dealt himself in.

Parker's eyes were now once again used to the light. As the guy turned away from the empty drawer in the bedside table, Parker stood, pushed open the door, and stepped into the room.

The guy saw him. His eyes focused, his body became still, and his right hand snaked inside his suit jacket, coming out with a small flat automatic. "Stop right there."

Not law, but close to law. "Don't be stupid," Parker told him, and spread his own empty hands. "Put that thing away, or I'll take it off you."

The guy ignored that. He waggled the gun toward the table and two chairs by the front door. "Sit down over there," he said.

"So you are stupid," Parker said, and walked toward him.

"Hey! Hey!" the guy said, startled, and backed up two steps to the wall. Then, before Parker could reach him, he holstered the automatic, just as rapidly as he'd taken it out. Showing his palms, he said, "All right."

Parker backed away, and now he was the one who pointed at the table and chairs, saying, "Why don't we both sit down?"

The guy frowned at him. "Jesus Christ," he

said thoughtfully. "What if I was the excitable type?"

"I'd calm you down," Parker told him. He went over and sat in the chair that didn't have its back to the door. Watching the guy, still standing there, indecisive, he said, "You're looking for the money."

The guy nodded, still frowning; not so much in agreement that he was looking for the money but accepting the force of the statement. "I know who I am," he said. "Who the hell are you?"

"John Orr," Parker told him. "Midwest Insurance."

"You're an *insurance man?*"

"Investigator."

"You got ID?"

"Never," Parker said. "Not on the job. How about you?"

Now at last the guy came over and sat in the other chair. He put one forearm on the table and said, "Dwayne Thorsen. Head of Security for the Christian Crusade."

"Archibald's guy."

"He's who I work for," Thorsen said. "You've got no ID on you at all?"

Parker pulled his wallet out of his hip pocket and dropped it on the table. "I've got papers on three different names in there," he said. "None of them true. It makes you feel better, look em over."

Thorsen looked at the beat-up wallet, then at Parker, and laughed. "You'll tell me when you're telling the truth," he said, "and you'll tell me when you're lying, and I can believe you or I can go fuck myself."

This was true, and there was no need for Parker to confirm it. There was a persona he wanted Thorsen to believe, and the more that persona was Thorsen's own invention, instead of a razzle-dazzle fed him by Parker, the better.

Thorsen said, "Midwest Insurance. Who's your client? The stadium?"

Parker put his wallet away. "Nobody," he said. "Not on this one."

Thorsen nodded, considering that. "What you mean is, you were already on their trail, for something else."

"One of them," Parker said. "A fellow named George Liss."

"That's a name I know," Thorsen agreed.

So Carmody had broken; not a surprise.

Thorsen went on, "Seems to be his real handle, Liss. What do you have on the others?"

"Nothing," Parker said. "They're not part of my job. Or they weren't. I guess they are now. Do you have names on them?"

"Not names I like," Thorsen said. "Jack Grant.

Ed and Brenda Fawcett." He waggled a hand, to show doubt. "That's what they told Carmody, for what it's worth."

Parker decided an insurance investigator following George Liss would have some knowledge of Carmody. He said, "Carmody. He's something in Liss's parole, isn't he?"

"He's also the inside man on the robbery," Thorsen said.

"It looked like there had to be somebody inside," Parker agreed. "And they holed up in that trailer that blew apart, I suppose."

"From there," Thorsen said, "God knows where they went."

"Who's running the investigation?"

Thorsen shook his head. "I don't like him," he said, "and you won't either. Detective Second Grade Calavecci."

"Is that why you're looking around here yourself? He's incompetent?"

"No, he's good at the job," Thorsen said. "I think the whole department's good. He just enjoys himself a little too much."

"Maybe I'll stay out of his way," Parker said.

"That's what I'm doing," Thorsen said. "Came over here to see what's what, when I couldn't stand him any more."

"You knew about this place from Carmody?"

"And also from another bunch, trying to cut

themselves a piece. Calavecci didn't want to come here, said they wouldn't be back, but you never know. Their stuff is here."

Parker said, "Another bunch?" That must be the trio in the car in the stadium parking lot. Who *were* those clowns? And where were they now? Parker said, "I don't know any other bunch."

"It's a sad story," Thorsen told him. "Carmody had a girlfriend. He told her what was going down here."

"Everybody talks to everybody," Parker said.

"They do," agreed Thorsen. "The girlfriend talked to her brother, who's an asshole. He talked to two other assholes he knew, and they decided to come hit the hitters."

"Did they," Parker said.

"Before they left," Thorsen went on, "the other two assholes went to see what else the sister might know, and killed her. Not meaning to, I guess."

Parker said, "The sister?"

"They didn't mention that part to the brother," Thorsen said. "They just all came here."

"To the motel, you mean. So they could follow the heisters."

"That's right."

"Liss told Carmody this was the motel, Carmody told the girlfriend, the girlfriend told the brother."

"As you say," Thorsen said, "everybody talks to everybody."

"The question is," Parker said, "who do I talk to?"

"The second bunch is in custody," Thorsen told him. "Calavecci was teasing the brother about the sister's death, not quite telling him, when I left."

"Uh huh."

"But I don't know that that bunch has much you want to know."

"They're nothing to me," Parker said. He was thinking, trying to find a way to turn this meeting into something useful. "I might want Carmody," he decided. "He could know associates of Liss, people Liss might go to if he has to go to ground."

"Calavecci and his people squeezed him pretty good, I think," Thorsen said.

"But they're thinking about the stadium, and the money. I'm thinking about Liss."

"That's true." Thorsen thought it over, and said, "I could phone, say we want to drop by—"

"You and the insurance man."

Thorsen grinned. "That's right. Just get an okay, a phone call from Calavecci to the hospital saying we're cleared to go in. That way, Calavecci won't have to come with us."

"He's a busy man anyway," Parker suggested.

Thorsen got to his feet. "I'll just make the call."

Also rising, Parker said, "Give me a minute in the john, and I'll be with you."

As Thorsen went over to the telephone on the bedside table, Parker went into the bathroom, shut the door, and looked through Brenda's cosmetics until he found a round black compact. He opened it, and the inside of the top was mirrored. With eyebrow pencil, he wrote on the mirror *11 PM*. Then he closed the compact and put it down a different place from where he'd found it, then flushed the toilet before leaving the room.

The one place he was sure Brenda would look was in a mirror.

4

Thorsen was still on the phone, saying, "Yeah," and, "I see," and, "How about that." He held a finger up toward Parker—one minute—and went on listening to the phone. Then he said, "Well, we'll come over and hang around until you're done," and hung up, and said, "I could grow to dislike that slimeball."

"The detective? Whatsisname?"

"Calavecci. He's waiting for the doctors to say he can go over and have a conversation with Carmody himself, probably by ten o'clock. When he's done, then we can go in."

The clock radio in the room read 9:23. "So we wait a while," Parker said.

"The thing is," Thorsen said, "what he's waiting to do. He wants to bring Quindero over

163

there, let him and Carmody have a conversation."

"Quindero?" This was a new name to Parker.

"The brother," Thorsen explained. "This is just the sadistic son of a bitch wanting to turn the knife a little more. Let Quindero and Carmody reminisce together about good old Mary."

"A nice guy, your detective."

"Let's get out of here," Thorsen said, looking around, disgusted. "There's more, I'll tell you in the car."

"Fine."

Thorsen nodded at the connecting door. "Nothing in there?"

"Same as here. They didn't leave any address books."

"These are not people with address books," Thorsen said. "Come along— What do I call you? John, or Jack?"

"Jack."

"And I'm Dwayne."

"Fine."

They went out, switching off the lights, and Thorsen said, "I parked across the street."

In the Professional Building parking lot, which was now half full. Thorsen's car was a rental, a blue Chevy Celebrity. He unlocked them into it, and on the console between the front seats was a black scanner, which he immediately switched on, saying, "I've got this fixed to the local police band. I'm not official, so Calavecci won't tell me anything unless I ask, and then he has to play around a little."

Thorsen had the volume low, so that the police dispatcher's voice was a raspy buzz that wouldn't interfere with conversation. Parker said, "There's more?"

Thorsen started the car, and drove out of the parking lot, and as they headed across the city he told Parker about the mess at the gas station this morning, and the kid hospitalized with a bullet in his leg, and the description of the station wagon and the duffel bags and the two men and a woman.

"The thing is," he finished, "my security people in the money room where it happened, they say it was three men. The kid's sure it was two men and a woman. During the robbery, the hitters had ski masks on, so maybe one of them was a woman all along."

"Wouldn't be the first time," Parker said.

"Then the other thing," Thorsen said. "Nobody knows if it's connected or not, but the locals have lost a cop. And his car."

Knowing this was Liss's work, Parker said, "Lost a cop? How do you mean?"

"The guy was on duty at an on-ramp someplace, by himself. When the relief showed up at six this morning, he and the car were gone. He doesn't respond to radio calls—you'll hear them, from time to time, they're still trying to raise him—and they don't know what it means."

"If the heisters have a police car," Parker said, "they could probably just drive on out of town and nobody think twice."

"Then why are they still in that gas station an hour later, with a station wagon? That's why nobody knows if it's connected."

"They'll find him," Parker said. "Their cop. Sooner or later. One way or another."

"What's driving them nuts is," Thorsen said, "if the hitters have that car, they've got the radio, just like this. They're listening to the pursuit."

"They're probably not enjoying it much," Parker said.

The hospital was well across town. Parker sat in the passenger seat as Thorsen drove from traffic light to traffic light, and the radio kept talking. From time to time, it called for an Officer Kendall, who never answered. Sometimes there was stuff about who would be on duty in and around the hospital, to guard Carmody. Then they found the station wagon.

Thorsen said, "What? Turn it up."

Parker turned it up, and they listened to the reports. A woman had reported her car stolen, a Toyota Tercel, from in front of her apartment building, discovering it when she went out to go to her morning class at the local college, and when the officers responded they found the battered station wagon in front of a fire hydrant directly across the street. So now the fugitives were presumed to be traveling in a dark green Toyota Tercel, license number S46 8TJ.

Except that Parker knew they weren't. He knew what Mackey would do now, because they'd both done it before, when they needed to buy time and they didn't dare travel in stolen wheels. Mackey and Brenda and the duffel bags, in the Toyota, would drive directly to a downtown parking garage, the kind where a machine gives you the ticket on the way in. There they'd park the Toyota, grab another car, wait in it twenty minutes or so, and pay on the way out with the ticket they'd got on the way in. This new car would take them to a motel, either the old one or more likely a new one. Once they had a room, Mackey would bring the new car back to where he'd got it, leave it there, and take a cab to the new hidey-hole.

Somewhere in this city. All Parker had to do was find them.

Up ahead, on the right, a patrolman strolled his beat, slow and relaxed, showing that not the entire local law was all caught up in the excitement. Parker saw him up ahead, from the back, saw how casual he was, then noticed how sloppy the uniform looked.

They drove by. Parker turned his head to look. It was Liss.

5

Stop? Get out of the car? Go after Liss right now?

No. Too complicated to strip away Thorsen. At this point, Thorsen was Parker's only way to find out what the law knew and what they were doing and whether or not anybody was close to Mackey and Brenda. There was time to reach out for Liss, if the law didn't scoop him up first. Carmody might know just the one thing that would lead Parker to Liss after this was all over. In the meantime, if Liss was killing time and nothing else, strolling around in the sunlight with his cop imitation, that meant he was just as far away as Parker from the duffel bags full of money. Liss could wait.

There was excitement at the hospital. Televi-

169

sion news vans, sprouting antennas like the whiskers on a witch's chin, lined both sides of the curved entrance road. Police vehicles took up the rest of the space in front, and cops were a heavy presence both inside and outside the main entrance. Thorsen left the Chevy in the very full visitors' parking lot, then talked himself and Parker into the main hospital building past any number of cops with questions, some of them local and some of them state. Everybody had to walkie-talkie to somebody else to get approval to let Thorsen through, but nobody questioned it when Thorsen vouched for Parker: Jack Orr, the insurance investigator.

In addition to Carmody, in a private room on four, there was also the kid from the gas station, Bill Trowbridge, in his own room on three. Trowbridge, having answered every question the cops could think of to ask, was now doing press and TV interviews and grinning like a goof at his mother, seated on an uncomfortable nearby chair, being firmly kept out of camera range. Among the reasons he gave for climbing the bins in the storage room and ripping his way through the roof, he did not mention his need to pee.

The hall leading from the elevator to Carmody was also full of cops. One of them, that Thorsen seemed to have met before, was a plainclothesman named Macready, who gave Parker a hello and a handshake at Thorsen's introduction, then said, "Lew's on his way here with Quindero. He wants everybody else to wait."

Thorsen said, "Not here yet?"

"The Quindero family's lobbed a lawyer in," Macready said. "It's delaying things a— Oh, here they are."

Out of an elevator and down the hall came a group of four, led by a big self-satisfied man who'd have to be Calavecci. Behind him came a skinny young scared guy with hands cuffed behind his back, and flanked by two serious-looking uniforms, each of them holding one of the cuffed guy's elbows. Parker looked at him past Calavecci and thought the young guy was probably one of the people from that car in the stadium parking lot.

But Calavecci was the point here. He said a smooth word to Thorsen, then was introduced to Jack Orr, insurance investigator. He shook hands too hard, grinned, and said, "So you've been chasing our boys longer'n we have."

"Just one," Parker said. "George Liss."

"A real piece of work," Calavecci said, with a pleased shake of the head. "I'm looking forward to a discussion with him. What a rap sheet."

"Yeah?"

"Got a record in the top ten," Calavecci said. "With a bullet. Why don't you and Dwayne wait in the dayroom over there, they got coffee and stuff for the nurses. We'll just have a little conversation, Ralph and me, with his pal Tom."

Parker saw that Ralph Quindero was trying not to cry. When he got in front of Carmody, he'd quit trying. They'd have a nice little tearfest in there, with Calavecci lapping it up, like a cat.

The dayroom was too bright, with fluorescents. A few nurses, trying to be cool but sneaking looks at the strangers, were clustered over coffee at a table in the corner. Thorsen and Parker got coffee of their own, both passing up the powdered near-milk, and carried the cardboard cups to another of the green Formica tables. They sat there in silence, waiting, the taste and smell of the coffee both a little obnoxious, and then Thorsen said, "This fella Liss."

"Yeah?"

"Does he work with a regular bunch? Same people all the time?"

"No," Parker said. "He isn't in a crew. He's too untrustworthy. He's just as likely to turn on his partners."

"Maybe he did this time," Thorsen said. "Maybe he's all any of us is looking for, at this point."

"Anything is possible," Parker agreed.

A few minutes later, Calavecci came in, got his own cup of coffee, and joined them at the table.

He seemed very content, as though he'd just had a good meal. "They're forgiving each other in there now," he said.

"That's nice," Thorsen said. He remained very flat and still when talking to Calavecci.

"I believe they're about to start praying for Mary's immortal soul," Calavecci went on, "so I left them in there with the guards. I'll go back in a few minutes." He gave Parker a measuring look. "You root around in the garbage a lot," he suggested.

"That's where the people are," Parker told him.

"You been chasing Liss a long time?"

"Eight months. He was part of a bank thing in Iowa City, took a hostage, killed her."

"What does the insurance company care?"

"They need Liss," Parker said, improvising from what he knew of previous situations, from the other side, "to prove the bank guards weren't incompetent. If they can prove the guards did what they were supposed to do, the company's liability goes way down."

Smiling pleasantly, Calavecci said, "And screw the survivors, right?"

Parker smiled back at him, just as pleasant and just as false. "That's the job," he said, and three shots sounded, flat and small but not far away. They could have been the sounds of somebody hitting a floor with a baseball bat, but they were not.

All three at the table knew it, and jumped to their feet. They were all moving toward the door before the first yells sounded outside. Calavecci went through the doorway, then Thorsen. Parker lagged, because he thought he knew what this was. He thought it wasn't a coincidence he'd seen George Liss walking toward the hospital.

Yes. The hall was full of armed men and women in blue, all facing the same way, frozen. Parker came through the doorway behind Thorsen and looked down the hall and Liss was backing away down there, waving the pistol he must have taken from the missing cop. He was still in the uniform, but what was protecting him now was Ralph Quindero. He backed away down the hall with Quindero in front of him, Liss's left arm tight around Quindero's waist, Quindero the shield, helplessly facing all those helpless armed people as he and Liss backed steadily away. There was a stairwell door back there, at the far end.

Liss, looking at everything, suddenly saw Parker, and laughed with surprise. "Well, look at you!" he cried, and fired at Parker's head.

6

Thorsen's lunge drove both Parker and himself back through the doorway into the dayroom, bouncing off the floor while the bullet hit the doorframe behind them. As they untangled themselves, there were sudden shouts from the hall, and a quick flurry of gunfire, almost immediately stopped.

Parker got to his feet as the uniforms in the hall rushed forward in a body, meaning Liss had made it to the stairwell. But how much farther could he go?

Parker turned and held out his hand to help Thorsen back to his feet. He said, "I owe you one."

Thorsen looked slightly ruffled, but then he

shook himself and became completely neat again. He said, "That was Liss, wasn't it?"

"It was."

"Looks like he knows you're behind him."

"Looks that way."

"And doesn't like it."

"I didn't think he would," Parker said, and started out of the room.

Thorsen, not moving, said, "Let the police run him down. Shouldn't take more than five minutes."

Over his shoulder, Parker said, "Carmody," and walked away down the now-deserted hall. Big eyes in shocked faces looked out from corners of cover at the nurse's station along the way.

Carmody's room was on the other side, just before the nurse's station. Parker went to that doorway and looked in, and it was a mess. Carmody had been shot in the head, and was lying back on the pillow, three eyes staring upward. The two cops who'd been in here with him, mostly to keep watch on Ralph Quindero, had been shot any which way, just to take them out of play, and were alive, but both lying like flung dolls on the floor, being worked over by nurses.

For Liss, Carmody was the only person except the rest of the crew who could positively say he'd been one of the heisters. It didn't matter if Carmody had given statements to the law, just so he wouldn't be around later to make the positive ID. Liss could afford a lawyer who'd fend off all that crap, dependent on there being no live Tom Carmody to stand up in court and point and say, "That's him there."

And what Liss was counting on right now, in the hospital, was too much confusion and nobody who'd ever seen him before. A guy in a police uniform, moving fast, shooting people, who came in and went out. There might be some potential IDs of Liss, but once again, not enough for a conviction. Not if he got away clean and hired his lawyer and established his alibi in some place like San Diego, or one of the Portlands.

"Gangway! Gangway!"

Parker stepped back, and white-coated people hurried by, pushing two gurneys into the room. Working delicately but hurriedly, moving fragile creatures who could break at any second, they put the two wounded cops on the gurneys.

Parker looked down the hall. Some of the cops had followed Liss into the stairwell, while others milled around down there, barking into walkie-talkies. Some had come the other way down the hall and were just now piling into an elevator. To go which way, up or down? Liss wouldn't be as easy to catch as these people thought.

Thorsen had also looked into Carmody's

room, and now he came over to Parker to say, "You can hold your questions."

"There's nothing for me here," Parker agreed. He was thinking, there was nothing for him around Thorsen any more, either. Get rid of him—maybe take him out of the action and borrow that little automatic of his—and then go find Mackey and Brenda. Liss was attracting too much attention right now, Parker didn't need to be around him.

Particularly since he was supposed to be the Liss expert, the insurance guy tracking him down. Calavecci had immediately gone running off to lead the search for Liss, but sooner or later he'd be back, and he'd be full of questions, and he'd probably even want to call Jack Orr's head office at Midwest Insurance, a company that so far as Parker knew didn't exist.

Down the hall, the plainclothesman called Macready came out of the stairwell and walked this way. Thorsen said, "Get him?"

"Not yet," Macready said.

Parker said, "You lost him."

"We know he's in the building," Macready said. "He isn't going anywhere." Frowning at Parker, he said, "He does seem to have a special interest in you, though, doesn't he?"

"We're interested in each other," Parker said. "He knows I don't mean him well."

An elevator door opened and cops came out. They looked both purposeful and confused, and they milled with the gurneys coming out of Carmody's room. Macready went over to talk to these new cops, and Parker said, "Time to get out of their way."

"As a matter of fact," Thorsen said, "I was just thinking the same. Come to the hotel."

Parker looked at him. "What hotel?"

"Archibald and the Crusade," Thorsen explained. "We're all supposed to leave town today, go back to Memphis, but it looks like at least some of us will be staying on. You and I can go there, phone Broad Street from time to time, find out what's going on."

A peaceful place. A good place to hole up until tonight; if nothing else happened, Parker could go back to that motel at eleven o'clock, see if Brenda'd been reading her compact lately. "Good idea," he said. "Thanks for the invite."

7

Macready rode down in the elevator with them. He had an air about him of gloomy satisfaction, as though taking pleasure in something he knew to be a sin. He said, "We got a situation here, I don't know if you two realize this."

Thorsen said, "A situation? What kind of situation?"

"I mean," Macready said, "Lew Calavecci went out on a limb when he brought the Quindero kid over here, and now maybe the limb broke off."

The elevator reached the ground floor. They stepped out to find a snag, a traffic jam of people being funneled slowly through one checkpoint at the main entrance. Everybody in and out was being closely studied.

Macready stood on line with them, and Thorsen asked him, "Out on a limb? Why?"

"What have they got Quindero on?" Macready asked. "Nothing, or next to nothing. His two pals killed the girl, his sister, but everybody acknowledges Quindero didn't know about it till long afterward, so he isn't a party to that crime at all. The three of them came here *intending* to commit a crime, but they didn't do it. The other two they're holding on murder one, to be shipped home, but all they have on Quindero, here or anywhere else, is obstruction of justice, because he knew the robbery at the stadium was going to take place and he didn't inform the police. But that's Mickey Mouse, and everybody knows it, that's just to hold onto him a couple days. His lawyer's going to laugh at that one. In fact, he's already laughing at it. But now we got a different situation."

Thorsen said, "What?"

Macready seemed to consider whether or not to go on. The line inched forward, people irritable but obedient, one at a time leaving the building, one at a time entering it. Macready said, "I don't know if you two got much of a sense of Lew Calavecci."

"I think we do," Thorsen said.

"Enough to go on," Parker said.

"Well," Macready told them, "Lew let Quindero believe he was in a lot deeper shit than he actually is. You know, he put the screws to him a little. More for fun than to get anything out of him. And he didn't get clearance from anybody to bring Quindero here to confront Carmody because he knew damn well nobody would *give* him clearance."

"Oh," said Thorsen.

"And now," Macready said, "it looks like Quindero's teamed up with our shooter."

Thorsen said, "Teamed up? He was a hostage."

"In the stairwell," Macready said, "the shooter took the time to shoot the lock on Quindero's cuffs, free him up. We found them there. Quindero must figure he's got nothing to lose, so he's thrown in with the shooter, and they're somewhere together. Two instead of one."

Parker said, "Calavecci needs Quindero back safe and sound, doesn't he? Not a scratch on him."

"Good luck, say I," said Macready. Looking at Parker, he said, "I hear the shooter was the guy you're looking for, is that right?"

"George Liss," Parker agreed. "Looked like him."

They were nearly to the head of the line; Macready would usher them through. Waiting, he nodded and said, "I can see where, following George Liss around, it wouldn't be dull work."

8

It wasn't a manger. Carlton Tower, where William Archibald and his Christian Crusade were resting their heads while they saved local souls, was a many-tiered wedding cake, white and gleaming in the sun, with the flags of various Scottish clans dangling from horizontal poles stuck out from the facade just above the second level. (Most people had no idea what those colorful flags stood for, and the few who did know couldn't figure out what they stood for *here*.)

The lobby was broad and two stories high, with a figured carpet in which the dominant color was maroon. The bank of gold-doored elevators stood discreetly around a corner on the right. Thorsen led the way across from the revolving-doored entrance, through an atmo-

sphere of hyper but hushed activity, and Parker
looked at it all with approval. He liked this kind
of place when he wasn't working. On the job, it
was no good, of course, because the byword with
a place like this was constant service of the guest,
which meant constant observation of the guest.
On the job, Parker preferred a place where,
once you paid your money and they told you
where the ice machine was, you were left alone.

Archibald and his people had taken all or
most of the twelfth floor. Thorsen and Parker
rode up in the elevator with blushing honey-
mooners, who continued on to greater heights.
When Thorsen and Parker stepped out of the elevator, they found a very neat and muscular
young man in dark gray suit and dark blue tie
seated on the nice wing chair against the opposite wall, reading what looked like a missal. He
glanced up, saw Thorsen, and said, "Morning,
sir."

"Morning. Archibald in?"

"I believe everybody's in, sir," the young man
said, and gave Parker a flat look, merely record-
ing him, to remember him. Parker already remembered the young man; he'd been one of the
Crusade's guards in the money room at the stadium.

Thorsen led the way down the hall, saying,
"We'll drop in, have a word with Archibald, then

go on to my office. He's an interesting fella to meet."

"I suppose he must be," Parker said.

They went to the end of the white-and-gold corridor, where the suites were, and Thorsen knocked on the door that instead of a number had the word *Macleod* on it. After a minute, this door was opened by another muscular youngster in a suit, a clone of the one at the elevator, though Parker didn't think this one had been in the money room.

Thorsen stepped in, murmuring a word to this guy, and Parker followed. They went through a small mirrored vestibule with two doors that probably led to closets, and then entered a large six-sided room with big windows in two walls showing cityscape. Paintings hung on the rest of the walls, cream-and-green broadloom was underfoot, and the furniture was large and dark, mostly imitation antique, and placed in separate groupings, the largest cluster being the two sofas and two chairs with several tables and lamps positioned in front of the now-idle fireplace. That detail surprised Parker; he'd thought Archibald would want a fire. Maybe too distracted by the loss of his money.

The remembered plummy voice from the night of the robbery oiled the room, coming from the man himself, seated at a small desk in front of the view, talking on the telephone. He gestured at Thorsen that he wouldn't be long, and went on with his conversation. Parker listened, and Archibald seemed to be on the line with his head office back in Memphis, arranging alterations in the television schedule created by the disruption that had happened here.

"Better coffee in this place," Thorsen said, and went over to the bar—from the doorway, it was fireplace to the left, bar to the right, Archibald on the phone straight ahead—where he filled two hotel china mugs with coffee from a glass pot on a warmer there. Parker joined him, hiking one hip onto a stool in front of the bar while Thorsen stood behind it, leaning against the back counter. The coffee was in fact much better than the stuff at the hospital.

Parker looked around. "Nice duty," he said.

Thorsen offered a thin smile. "Depends what you like."

When Archibald got off the phone, everybody moved, Archibald rising and turning his smile toward the room as though it contained multitudes, Parker getting to his feet and standing there with the coffee mug in his left hand, Thorsen coming around the end of the bar to make the introductions. "Reverend William Archibald," he said, as the three moved toward one another, "may I present Mr. John Orr, an undercover insurance investigator from Midwest Insurance."

Archibald's handshake was firm but not aggressive. "Mr. Orr," he said, in greeting. "Here concerning our unfortunate loss?"

"Not exactly," Parker said.

Thorsen said, "Mr. Orr was on another case. He was already in pursuit of one of the fellas robbed us, for something else he did."

Archibald smiled, with ruefulness in it. "In that case, Mr. Orr," he said, "I can only regret that you didn't catch up with him last week."

"I feel the same way," Parker told him.

"But now you're here," Archibald said, "I presume you've taken our misfortune under your wing as well."

"That would be a different insurance company," Parker said.

Thorsen said, "Mr. Orr's got a full plate, Will. This fella he's after is a very bad man. Just caused a ruckus down at Memorial Hospital." His voice lowered, becoming as funereal as his boss, as he said, "I'm afraid Tom Carmody's dead."

That startled Archibald. "Why, that's terrible!" Looking at Parker, he said, "Tom was one of my failures, Mr. Orr. I'm not going to get over this."

"Uh huh," Parker said.

"But at least," Archibald said, brightening, "he

expressed sorrow for his wayward ways. Toward the end, Dwayne, didn't he? You were there."

"He was sorry, all right," Thorsen said.

"We'll remember him in our prayers," Archibald decided.

A blonde woman came into the room, then, from somewhere deeper in the suite, and attracted everybody's attention; which is what she would do in any room she entered. Ripe to overflowing, she was almost a parody of the sexpot, but kept under strict control, her yellow hair in a tight bun, lush body completely covered in a sexless gray suit and high-necked white blouse, and dark horn-rim glasses worn to distract from the bee-stung mouth.

Archibald's smile when he turned to greet her contained the avarice of ownership; not much question who this woman was. "Ah, Tina," the Reverend said. "Come meet Mr. Orr. He leads a very exciting life."

When she came forward, Parker could see her rein herself in, deliberately hold herself within tight bounds. Her smile was small, almost prissy, and she didn't quite meet his eye as she murmured, "Does he? How nice."

"Mr. John Orr," Archibald said, presenting his proudest possession, "Ms. Christine Mackenzie, conductor of our Angel Choir."

"How do you do?"

Her hand was soft, with toughness within. Holding Parker's a second too long, she said, "What about your life makes it so exciting, Mr. Orr?"

"Not much," Parker told her.

Archibald said, "Mr. Orr's an undercover detective, working for an insurance company."

"*Are* you?" The smile opened a bit more, showed a gleam of teeth. "You must have some stories to tell."

"Mostly, I keep them to myself," Parker said.

He'd been aware of the transformation of Thorsen since Christine Mackenzie had come into the room. The man reacted with barely concealed rage and revulsion, covering panic; the sexuality of this woman was clearly far more than Thorsen could take. He wanted out of here, and now, gruffly, without looking at the woman, he said, "Will, Mr. Orr and I are going to my office, call Broad Street, find out if there's any developments."

"Broad Street." Archibald frowned slightly. "That's what they call their police headquarters here?"

"They better not ever move it," Christine Mackenzie said, and giggled, and showed Parker her tongue.

Thorsen turned away, his hands clenched into fists. "Come on, Jack," he said.

"Nice to meet you," Parker told Archibald, and nodded to Mackenzie. "Both of you."

But Archibald said, "Dwayne, you go ahead. Let me have a little word with Mr. Orr, if I might. I'll send him right along."

"Fine," Thorsen said. To Parker he said, "I'm down on the right, 1237."

"Got it."

Thorsen left, and Archibald said, "More coffee, Mr. Orr?"

"No, I'm fine."

Archibald turned to Mackenzie, saying, "Tina, go in the other room, please, and phone the concierge, and ask for somebody to come up and lay a fire, would you do that, please?"

She would rather stay, but that wasn't being given as a choice. "All right," she said, with a shrug that made her breasts call attention to themselves, even within all that nunnery. Approaching Parker, "Glad to meet you," she said, with another smile, and offered her hand once more. "I hope we meet again."

"That'd be nice," Parker assured her.

Archibald was impatient for her to leave, and was making it increasingly obvious. Now, he said, "I'll be along after a while, Tina."

Which meant don't come back, a message Tina understood. She rolled her eyes discreetly at Parker, and went away, and twitched just a little as she left.

Archibald said, "Mr. Orr, sit down a minute, won't you?"

They sat on sofas at right angles to one another near the fireplace, toward which Archibald sent a fretful look, saying, "I meant to call someone, have them lay a fire in there, but I just haven't had a minute to myself." Smiling at Parker in amused self-pity, he said, "I do think a fire cheers up a room, at any season. Don't you?"

"Sure."

"What I wanted to talk about," Archibald said, hunched forward slightly, becoming more confidential, "is your job. You're a sort of undercover policeman, aren't you? But with the insurance company, not the regular police."

"Something like that."

"You have . . . contacts within the underworld, different from what the police might have."

"I'm supposed to, anyway," Parker said.

"People like you," Archibald said, "people in your position, they do moonlight, I believe, from time to time. Isn't that what it's called? To moonlight?"

"You mean collect from two bosses for the same work."

"Well, slightly different work," Archibald corrected him. "Similar work. For instance, you're looking for this one man anyway, but my understanding is, there were at least three involved in the robbery at the stadium, and probably a fourth man to drive them away. When you catch the man you're looking for, and I have no doubt that you're very able at your job, that you will run this fellow to earth, but when you do, it's extremely unlikely he'll have all the money from that robbery on his person."

"Very unlikely," Parker agreed.

"If you could make it a part of your business," Archibald said, looking Parker forthrightly in the eye, "to retrieve the money stolen from me, whether it's in the possession of the man you're hunting or not, I'd be very appreciative."

"Would you," Parker said.

"I'd pay in cash, of course."

"Uh huh."

"And you ought to have— What do they call it in your business? A retainer?"

"That's one word," Parker agreed.

"Let's say a thousand." Getting to his feet, not waiting for an answer, Archibald turned toward the desk where he'd been on the phone before. Crossing to it, he said over his shoulder, "Against, let us say, five percent of whatever you reclaim. That's a maximum of twenty-five thousand dollars, Mr. Orr, or just a little less."

Parker got to his feet and watched. Archibald

opened a drawer in the desk, took out a thick envelope that seemed to be full of cash, thumbed some bills out, and put the still-full envelope back in the drawer. Then he took up the bills he'd selected, slipped them into a hotel envelope, and came smiling back, envelope held out. "An extra little blessing on your job," he said. "Shall we call it that?"

This was the first time Parker had ever been offered a bribe to help find the money he'd stolen. "Let's call it that," he said, and took the envelope and put it in his pocket.

9

Thorsen's office was converted from a normal hotel room. The wall-to-wall carpet showed indentations where the bed's wheels had been and the feet of the other furniture, all of which had been taken out and replaced by two desks, four office chairs and a number of telephones. The connecting door to the next room was slightly ajar; Parker guessed that was where Thorsen slept.

When he came in, Thorsen was at the desk nearer the window, just finishing a phone conversation. It didn't seem to be pleasing him. He said one or two brief things, and then he said, "Thanks," sounding sour, and hung up. "Sit down," he told Parker, gesturing toward the chair at the other desk. "Your guy Liss got away."

"Uh huh," Parker said, and took the seat offered. Both desks were gray metal, basic models. The one he sat at had nothing on its surface, and probably nothing in its drawers.

Thorsen said, "You don't sound surprised."

"I'm not. How'd he do it? Is the other one still with him?"

"Quindero? Oh, yes. Calavecci is not a happy man."

"Quindero," Parker suggested, "thinks he must be a desperate criminal, with nothing to lose."

"And he isn't," Thorsen said. "But by the time this is over, he probably will be. Or dead."

"How did Liss get out?"

"The hospital morgue is in the basement," Thorsen told him. "There's a special back way in, unobtrusive, from a side street, with a ramp, for the hearses from the different morticians. They don't like dead bodies and hearses around the front, gives the wrong image, looks like failure."

Parker said, "So the two of them went down there."

"Where a body was being loaded. The hearse driver and a morgue attendant. I guess Liss didn't want to make too much noise, which was lucky for those two guys, because he just concussed them and tied them up. Then he and Quindero and the hearse—and the body, just to get even more people upset—went up the ramp and through a shit-poor roadblock there, and disappeared."

"And now," Parker said, "Quindero has committed a felony."

"He has, hasn't he? This mess is not getting neater," Thorsen said. "Did Archibald offer to pay you to find his cash?"

"A thousand now, one percent later."

"Did you take it?"

"It was impolite not to," Parker said.

"That's true. Excuse me," Thorsen said, and turned away to one of his phones. He pressed four numbers, so it was a call inside the hotel. "Okay," he said, and hung up.

So it was going to be like that. Parker turned toward the slightly open connecting door, and in came four more of Thorsen's young troops, of the same standard issue: Dark suits, dark ties, dark shoes, white shirts, close-cropped hair, expressionless faces. They would do well at taking orders, and they would do well at giving orders, too. Parker smiled at them, then looked at Thorsen. "And I thought we were getting along pretty good," he said.

"Now, whoever you are," Thorsen said, with no friendliness in it at all, "let's hear your real story."

10

What was it you didn't like about my story so far?"

"Everything," Thorsen said. "But to tell you the truth, and it's humiliating to say this, simple fuck that I am, I bought it for a while. Jack Orr, daredevil insurance spy." He shook his head, discouraged with himself.

"Go on buying it," Parker suggested. "It's nice, and it's true, and it's the only story I've got."

"We'll change your mind on that pretty quick," Thorsen said.

The four young guys all shifted position and moved their shoulders around, like a herd that had just caught a whiff of something on the breeze. Parker looked at them, and then back at Thorsen, who said, "Let me tell you when I finally got to singing in time with the chorus. It was when your friend Liss took a shot at you."

"He knows who I am," Parker pointed out. "He knows I'm after him."

"Everybody in that hall was after him," Thorsen said. "He didn't need to bust his own concentration to even some old scores. You said it yourself: He came there because Tom Carmody and the other robbers were the only people who could place him absolutely at the robbery, and he doesn't want anybody around who can do that. So he killed Tom, and the only other person he tried to kill was you."

Parker grinned, as though Thorsen must either be kidding or crazy. "Making me one of the heisters?"

"Heisters," Thorsen echoed. "That's a crook's word for it. We say robbers, or hitters."

"Crooks are who I hang out with."

"I'll tell you what happened," Thorsen said, ignoring that. "After the robbery, you all got split up somehow. One bunch spent the night in that gas station. Liss stole that police car and probably killed the poor cop. And you waited at the motel, until I showed up."

"Wait a second," Parker said. "Am I a heister, am I a robber, or am I a guy waiting at the motel?"

"I figure the details have to come from you," Thorsen told him.

Parker shook his head. "It's your fairy tale," he said, "you'll have to fill it in yourself. George Liss takes one shot at the guy been chasing him eight months, and to you that means the guy's in on the heist."

"That shot," Thorsen said, "made me start to think about something that had snagged me but I'd just let it go by. You know what that was?"

"You'll tell me," Parker said.

"There's a lot of different words for the room that, when I was in the Marines, we called the head. There's the bathroom, the toilet, the lavatory, the washroom, the WC. The Irish call it the bog. I've been places they called it the cloakroom, don't ask me why. But one thing is constant and sure and solid and you could build your house on it: Nobody named John calls that room the john."

Parker nodded. "I think you're right about that."

"So that isn't your name."

"That's my joke," Parker told him. "My name is John Orr. Meaning, my name is John, or it isn't."

"It isn't. You're one of the robbers. You and Liss had a falling-out." Thorsen showed that thin smile again, thinner than ever. "I think Liss makes a career out of having falling-outs with people. I think maybe he doesn't play well with others. What do you think?"

Parker said, "Dwayne, I understand, the situation you're in, it can make you jumpy, paranoid. The story I told you is solid."

"Then I'm gonna owe you an apology," Thorsen said. "But before I give you that apology, let's take a picture of you, and take your fingerprints, and ask the local law to check you out. And let's call your home office in— Where's Midwest Insurance located, by the way? I called our insurance guy in Memphis just now, and he never heard of it."

"That's because he's in Memphis. He isn't in the midwest."

Thorsen poised a hotel pen over a hotel notepad. "Give me the phone number of your home office, and the name of your supervisor." When Parker didn't say anything, he smiled again and said, "And you might as well also give me the Reverend's thousand dollars, while you're at it."

So this piece was played out. Parker glanced around at the four young guys standing there at parade rest, silent, watching, ready to do whatever they were told. He said, "Are these guys armed?"

"You don't want to know," Thorsen said.

"Oh, yes, I do. I've been without a gun for too long, I need one. I'm wondering, do I take that dinky thing of yours, or is one of these fellas better hipped?"

One of the youngsters spoke: "We don't need to be armed," he said, being tough.

Thorsen had put the pen down to stare at Parker. "By God, you're sure of yourself," he said.

"Why not," Parker said, and rose from the desk. As he did so, he pulled the empty metal side drawer out of the desk and swung it around in a short quick arc into Thorsen's face.

11

Always take out the brains first. Then you can deal with the hands and feet.

The four guys hadn't known it was going to play out like this. They'd thought their presence was supposed to keep trouble from happening. They were still working on their poses when Parker moved, so they were still reacting when Parker finished his first lunge, halfway across Thorsen's desk, Thorsen flying backward out of his chair, his face a red mess.

The return swing with the metal drawer caught the nearest young lion on the side of the head, and sent him reeling into number two, while Parker ran forward, the drawer held out in front of him like a battering ram, and caught number three as he was trying to duck away. One bottom corner of the drawer sliced his cheek as the other corner gouged his shoulder, and the whole drawer, Parker's momentum behind it, drove him straight back into the wall. He hit hard, crunched between the wall and Parker's weight on the drawer, and he dropped straight down when Parker let go of the drawer. The drawer and the man were both still falling when Parker spun around and kicked number four twice, first in the balls and then in the forehead as, in agony, he bent quickly down.

These four had trained in gyms, and knew a lot about self-defense. They actually didn't have guns, and they'd never thought they would need such help. But they'd never been crowded into a small room before, getting in each other's way, with somebody who was trying to kill them and who didn't do any of the moves they'd learned about in gym.

Thorsen and numbers three and four were out of play. Number one, having been side-swiped with the drawer, was groggy but standing, and number two was moving in on Parker, hands splayed out, doing *all* the moves he'd learned.

Parker didn't have a lot of time. He didn't know how much noise he was making or who might be around to hear it. He didn't know when it would occur to one of these survivors to run the hell out of this room and go for help. He didn't know when it would be too late to get out of here, so he had to get out of here *now,* so he lunged in, ducked back, feinted for the balls, and sliced the edge of his left hand across number two's Adam's apple. Number two stopped, clutched his throat, made a strangled scream, and fell backward, trying desperately to breathe.

Number one, bleeding on the side of the head where the drawer had hit him, was getting less groggy by the second, but wasn't yet one hundred percent. He came in at Parker, arms in defensive position, looking to throw a punch, and Parker pointed at number two, on the floor, making terrible noises through his crushed throat: "If I put you down, there won't be anybody around to get him breathing."

Number one looked down and to his right, following the point of the finger and the sounds from his friend, and Parker stepped in fast to clip the side of that jaw with his right elbow.

Forty seconds since he'd first reached for the drawer. They were all down. They were all out and silent except the one trying to breathe. Parker crossed to Thorsen, stripped off the coat, stripped off the very nice holster that was engineered to fit against the side without a strap across the body, and put it on himself, under his jacket. It would need some adjustment later, but it would do for now.

12

The hall was empty. Parker pulled the door to 1237 hard shut, to lock it, and walked at a steady pace toward the turn to the elevators. Behind him, way back at or near Archibald's suite, a door opened and closed, but he didn't look back.

The neat young guard was still in place on the wing chair facing the elevators. He nodded when Parker came around the corner, and put a finger in his missal to hold his place. Parker said, "How you doin?"

"Fine, sir."

Parker pushed the Down button and waited, but before it arrived someone else came walking around the corner. Christine Mackenzie. Dressed as before, but now with a simple gray hat and

gray cloak as well, as though she were on her way
to give alms to the poor. "Well, hello," she said,
on seeing Parker, with a bigger smile than she'd
permitted herself back in the suite. "Fancy meeting you here," as though she hadn't been watching Thorsen's office door, waiting for him to
leave.

"How you doing?" Parker said.

"Well, I'm doing fine," she told him. "Since we
have this unexpected stay here in this nice city, I
believe I'm going to do some shopping."

"Good idea."

The elevator arrived. He gestured, and she
boarded, and he boarded, and she pushed L.
The young guard was back reading his missal
again before the doors closed.

They were alone in the elevator. "You should
see the view on nine," she said, and pushed that
button.

Parker didn't have time for views, or anything
else. A lot of people were going to be chasing
after him in a few minutes. He said, "Why's that
better than the view on twelve?"

Here they were at nine already. "They have a
conference room here," she said, holding the
door open. "Huge windows, all around. Come
on and see, it's fabulous."

It was easier to go along. "Okay," he said, following her out of the elevator. "Show it to me."

She giggled, a low contralto. "I will," she said.

He never thought about sex when he was working, but he was always hungry for it afterward. What situation was this he was in now? The heist was done, and yet it wasn't done. The job was finished, but it was still going on, with complications and trailing smoke. Was he going to have sex with this woman now, or not? He looked at her body, imperfectly hidden in somebody else's clothing, and it looked very good, but his mind kept filling with Liss, with Brenda and Mackey, with the duffel bags full of money; and now with Thorsen and Archibald and Calavecci and Quindero and who knew how many more. But still, it was a good body, walking along beside him here.

The conference room was at the opposite end on nine from Archibald's suite on twelve, so it was a view of a different quadrant of the city, but not that much different. Still, the room was large and airy and empty, with thick gray-green carpet and a large free-form conference table and some tan leatherette sofas along the inner wall.

"Come look," she said, and when he went over to stand beside her she hooked her arm through his. "I love the way the sunlight bounces off that roof," she said, pointing with her free hand. "See it?"

"Yes."

She smiled at him, came close to laughing at him. "You don't care much for views, do you?"

"Depends," he said, and bit that swollen lower lip.

"Oo, careful," she said. "No marks."

Beneath his hand, her breast was so firmly contained in place it might have been made of kapok. This wasn't going to work; she might as well be a sofa. "Not a good idea," he said, and backed away, disengaging her arm.

"You don't think so?" She stood by the window, facing him, letting the full light from outside make her argument.

Three floors up, they'd surely be making phone calls by now, and not all of them for a doctor. Parker said, "Sometimes the time isn't the right time."

"All times are the right time," she corrected him, and slowly smiled. "As the Bible says, Hope deferred maketh the heart sick."

"That's the Bible?"

"I always do what the Bible tells me," she said, and stretched, and smiled again. "Come, let us take our fill of love, until the morning. It says that, too."

She was a true pistol. He said, "What about Archibald?"

She laughed at the idea that he cared about

Archibald. "Stolen waters are sweet," she quoted, "and bread eaten in secret is pleasant."

"I'm sure it is," Parker told her. "And it'll be even better later. I'll take a rain check."

The smile disappeared. The body snapped to attention. Behind the horn-rim glasses, the blue eyes flashed at him. "Rain check? I'm not a *game*."

That wasn't from the Bible.

FOUR

1

It was called Sherenden, and it was a house from the twenties, modern architecture of the time, designed by someone famous in his day and built at the edge of a ravine in what had then been the outskirts of town. On two steep acres of brush-covered rocky hill, at the end of a narrow winding road from the nearest city avenue, the house had been constructed of fieldstone and native woods and stainless steel, fitted into the broken shape of the landscape, with a large airy living room at the top, four windowed walls around a central black-stone fireplace. The rest of the house spread away beneath, for a total of four stories with an interior elevator, its shaft blasted into the rock.

The original owner was a lawyer, also famous

in his day, and the bottom level of the house, en-closed by two jutting rock ledges of ravine, had been his study, with accompanying bath and small kitchen. From his desk in there he could look out through plate glass at the wildness of his ravine as though suspended from a balloon, and not see the slightest corner of the rest of the house.

When it was built, the place was considered daring and original and one of the templates that would describe the future. It was written up approvingly in newspapers and magazines of its day, and was still mentioned, with small black-and-white photos, in books on modern architec-ture.

Time had not been kind to the house. First there had been the divorce, as acrimonious as any divorce in the history of law, which had seen Sherenden fought over but unlived in for more than ten years. The winner, the ex-wife, had had no real use for the house but had wanted it out of spite, and had thereafter ignored it almost completely. Her heirs sold it as soon as they could.

Then there was the city, which had grown in ways and directions not expected by the town planners. This rocky area just within the city lim-its, full of inaccessible ravines, had seemed the least likely direction for the city to grow. But then, after World War Two, the interstate high-way system was born, and an on-ramp was placed just outside the city line in this direction, and it suddenly made sense to knock down hills and fill ravines and put in working-class housing developments; a thousand homes from the same blue-print, girdling the two acres that contained Sherenden.

In the early sixties, one of the subsequent owners turned Sherenden into two apartments, by means of a lot of plywood and the removal of about half the original windows. (The elevator had ceased to function years before, and now became an additional closet on each level.) In the late seventies, another owner decided to restore the place to its former glory, despite the fact that the views from the living room were now of many small Monopoly-board houses stretching away toward infinity and the view from the bottom floor study was of the dump that had been made at the base of the ravine. However, he went bankrupt while the work was still under way, and so the plywood went back up, even more than before, sealing the house away.

The bank that took over at that point enclosed Sherenden with a tall wire fence, and waited. They were always on the verge of selling the two acres—nobody at the bank ever thought about the house itself, except as a problem—to someone who would demolish the "existing structure" and level the land and put in eight houses, but the deals always fell through.

Kids and vagrants and drunks had made a sieve of the fence and a sty of the house. In the last decade, homeowners in Golden Heights and Oak Valley Ridge Estates, the neighboring development communities, had put forth a number of petitions against this eyesore in their midst, but the bank wouldn't tear the place down without a purchaser, and so the stalemate continued.

2

Parker took a cab to a shopping center, out away from the middle of town. He had lunch in a bar there—despite its fake Tiffany lamps, it was a bar—and watched the television up on its high shelf, full of excited local bulletins, one after another. A whole lot of stuff happening around here these days. The bartender thought it was probably the work of a private army, stocking up money and supplies for the revolution, and Parker said he thought the guy was right. The bartender had known after one look that Parker was a kindred spirit.

From the phone booth in the back of the bar, Parker called the Midway Motel and asked for Mr. or Mrs. Fawcett, and was told they'd checked out. No, the woman on the phone didn't know when they'd left, they were just gone. He asked to be connected to Mr. Grant's room, and let the phone ring in the black emptiness there for a good long time. The woman who'd switched him over never did come back to tell him his party wasn't answering and might be out and did he want to leave a message, so eventually he hung up.

Brenda had her compact, anyway. And Liss was probably not at the motel. Was he at the house, he and Quindero?

A city bus line ran past this shopping center and on out to the developments by the interstate. Parker took it, at two-thirty that afternoon, a time when the passengers were a few schoolkids getting home early, some maids and cleaning women done with their day's work, and shoppers sitting slumped in the middle of their mounds of parcels.

Parker left the bus at the first corner in Oak Valley Ridge Estates and walked back down Oak Valley Ridge Avenue the way he'd come. In just over a hundred yards he got to the road leading in to the right. A pair of crumbling stone pillars, once graceful but now anemic, with bad rusted gouges at the top where the light fixtures had long ago been stolen, flanked a blacktop road that immediately curved down and away to the right, disappearing into a tangle of shrubs and trees. Wild rose vines knitted the underbrush to-gether, interweaving their tough thorny stalks with the tamer junipers and maples, making it impossible for a human being to travel anywhere in there except on the road.

The road itself was receding back to nature. Frosts and rain had crumbled the blacktop, and weeds had grown through. Branches encroached from both sides, and closed completely over the top. Nothing here invited the passerby, and in fact the passerby was told to go away. PRIVATE PROPERTY NO ENTRY said the black letters on the yellow metal sign hung from the thick chain arced between the pillars. NO TRESPASSING said the black letters on the yellow plastic sign sta-pled to the pillar on the left, and DANGER KEEP OUT said the red and black letters on the white plastic sign stapled to the pillar on the right.

Parker slowed as he neared this welcome, wait-ing for two cars to finish going by. They did, and he stepped over the chain and walked briskly down the first curving slope.

He was now on the bank's two acres, an irreg-ularly shaped parcel lying like a throw rug atop a lumpily unmade bed. The blacktop, almost dis-appearing in places, curved and climbed and dipped, covering nearly a quarter of a mile in what would have been much less distance in a straight flat line from entrance to house. Along the way, he saw nothing but shrubs and trees and vines, and at one point the faded blue trunk of a car that someone had years ago driven or pushed off the road into a deeper spot. The undergrowth grew up through the car, as though it weren't there.

In the old days, the first view of the house must have been something. You climbed a steep slope, came around a corner, and there in front of you was a wall of glass. Inside were the lights, and the graceful lines of the furniture, and the glow of the fireplace, and the confident movements of people. And beyond all that, seen through the house, was the view, already visible from here, of wild nature, tumbled scenery, and open sky.

Today there was the fence; that was the first thing. Eight feet high, chain link, it had one of its vertical metal support bars sunk into the middle of the road itself, to declare this no longer a road. Beyond the fence was the wall of plywood, darkened and discolored by time. It didn't look like a house any more. It didn't look like anything.

The fence had been snipped at the right edge of the roadway, as though for a prisoner-of-war escape, just enough to make it possible to push the flap of fence back out of the way and ease slowly through without ripping your clothes;

though sometimes, to judge by the frayed threads on some of the sliced-off edges, clothes did get caught here.

Parker eased his way through, and moved to the right, over weedy ground that had once been lawn and had not yet been completely reclaimed by woods.

He'd been here before, with Mackey and Liss, when they'd been making ready for the job. It was Mackey who'd found the place, and researched it in architecture books in the library, and was as proud of it as if he'd designed it himself. "Parker, it's a beauty. Nobody knows it's there, you got a million hiding places inside it, and it's right next to the entrance to the interstate!"

At first, Parker wasn't so sure. He had never liked places with only one entrance and exit. Given the situation with this house, once you were in it, the only way out was back that same road. On both sides of the house were woods that would eat you alive, and behind it was the ravine, too deep to get into and too steep to get out of, being very slowly filled as a town dump.

But Mackey was right about one thing: the house did have more than its share of hiding places for a few duffel bags. And they didn't intend to stay there at all, just drop the loot and go back to the motel. The idea was, if it so happened that any of them *was* made, or questioned, or shaken down by the cops, the swag would be nowhere near them.

So they'd gone through the house, Mackey leading the way, and it was Mackey who'd pointed out that there used to be an elevator in here where these closets were, and that its motor had been at the bottom of the shaft. The floors in all the closets that had been installed after the elevator car itself was removed and sold were plywood, and would pry up very easily. Mackey showed them how easy it would be to pry up the floor in the bottom-level closet, which revealed the old black motor, furred with dust on grease, leaving plenty of room for the duffel bags. It did mean lugging the bags down three flights of stairs and later back up again, but they would certainly be safe down in there for a few days.

If things had gone right.

Now Parker needed a place to lie low until tonight, when he could steal a car from the nearby development and go see if Brenda had caught up on her reading. At the moment, there were too many people looking for him, people who knew his face if nothing else about him. He had to give up the idea of settling with Liss until this whole operation was finished; unless Liss had also decided to hole up at the house.

Of course, the house still had its same disadvantage: one way in, one way out. But that could be an advantage, too. From inside the house, Parker could watch the road. If he saw anybody coming in, he might not be able to leave, but at least he'd know about them before they knew about him.

The loosened plywood, the new entry, was at the left corner of the house, near where the original front door had been. Parker looked over his shoulder, saw nothing, and eased inside.

3

The plywood sheathing made the interior dark, but cracks and spaces here and there provided some dim uneven light, in which Parker could see the truncated living room. A wall had been run across from front to back just beyond the fireplace, dividing the space in two, with the larger half out here. Later, the fireplace had been dismantled and covered over, leaving only a conical half dunce cap jutting for no apparent reason out of this new wall at chest height. The doors that had once been installed in the new wall were long gone. There was no furniture left in here, but rags and cans and bottles littered the floor.

The structure was still solid, having been built for a longer life than it was getting. When Parker crossed the living room, the floor neither squeaked nor sagged. He moved silently, a shadow in the shadows, to the nearer door in the new wall, which led to the kitchen that had been installed when this place became a duplex.

The kitchen equipment was now gone, leaving only holes in wall and floor with stubs of pipe where the plumbing had been. The elevator, on this level, had become a pantry, which now gaped open, doorless and empty. Near it was a spot where the outer sheathing of plywood didn't quite meet the original stainless steel corner post, leaving about an inch of unimpeded glass from top to bottom. Rain-streaked on the outside, the glass was still clear enough to see through, with the chain-link fence a silver grid in the afternoon sunlight out front, defining the location of the road.

Parker went over to that corner to lean close and look through, and saw nothing but the crowding woods and empty road. Then he stepped back, to study the glass itself, which was dusty and streaked all along here, its dirtiness hard to see because the plywood outside was flush against it. But the narrow band not covered by plywood was easier to look at, and just at eye level it had been roughly cleaned. The side of a hand, or maybe one of the rags from the floor here, had swept across the glass at just the right height for somebody to look out.

When was that done? Weeks ago, when Mackey first came to the place, before he brought Parker and Liss out? Earlier, or later, by somebody else completely, some vagrant or drunk just passing through? Or very recently?

Parker stood absolutely still for a long time, listening, alert, waiting. Facing the road as he was, he stood at the rear left side of the house, with the large living room making a C-shape to his right, around a central core. At his back was a wall separating this space from an interior coat-room and wet bar, its doorless doorway directly behind him. At the right end of that wall was the staircase, open to the living room up here, that went downward, flanked by interior walls, into the rear of the dining room one level below. To his left was the remnant of wall and the second smaller staircase that had been put in when the house was divided into two.

Not a sound in the house, nothing to be heard, not anywhere. Would he be able to hear people on the lower levels? Would they have heard him? The house was solid, even if very open, with these stairwells and open-plan rooms. What could be heard in here?

Very slowly his concentration shifted. There was still nothing to be heard, but he'd become aware of something else. Something very faintly in the air, something he could smell. Just a hint on the air, but it had to be very recent. A homely smell, almost a joke, but a warning.

Pizza.

4

They're in here, Parker thought. Liss and Quindero. They would have seen me coming. Standing here, watching, eating the pizza they'd brought in. And now they're waiting. Liss didn't shoot, as I came in the door.

What are they waiting for? To see if Mackey is with me? No. To lead them to the money.

Parker stayed motionless. He seemed to be looking out at the fence and the road, but his attention was inward and behind him, and he was thinking. Liss had tried to kill him at the hospital, but was waiting now. Why? Because, at the hospital, for all Liss knew Parker had already been caught, and could be expected to trade Liss for lighter treatment for himself. But here and now, with Parker not in the hands of the law, and with the money not in Liss's hands, Liss wouldn't want to kill him. Not yet. Not until he had the duffel bags.

Where is he? Where's his new ball boy, the punk Quindero? Either he's hoping to stay out of sight and wait for me to leave, and then follow me to the money, meaning he's down a couple of flights right now, staying well out of the way, or he's close, in the room behind this one, wanting to make a move, waiting only to be sure I'm alone.

That was the way to play it. Liss hovering, just out of sight, the way he did last night. Softly, not turning around, speaking in a conversational way as though the discussion had been going on for some time, Parker said, "Well, George, here we are."

Nothing. No response. Parker focused on the outside world, where nothing had changed. In the same easy tone, he said, "Everybody makes mistakes. But then we move on."

Still nothing. Maybe he really was alone in here, but he didn't believe it. "George," he said, "we can go on making trouble for each other, but that way we both lose, and Ed Mackey takes home the whole jackpot. Or we can go back to the original idea, three guys, three splits."

"What do I need you for?"

The voice was very faint, with that slur in it

caused by the dead half of Liss's face. It came from well back, probably the doorway to the interior room. Parker didn't smile, but he relaxed, because he knew now everything would be all right. He'd kill Liss when the time came, and Brenda and Mackey would be waiting for him at eleven o'clock and all would be well. Still not turning, he said, "George, you know what you need me for. Without me, you'll never see the money."

"You know where it is?"

"Not now. I know where it's going to be."

"When?"

"Twelve tonight."

"Where?"

Parker shook his head, and smiled at the narrow view between the plywood and the stainless steel. "George," he said, "why do you want me to lie to you?"

"We'll all go there together, is that the idea? At twelve?"

"All?"

"I've got a new partner."

So Quindero was with him back there. Liss wouldn't call him a partner out of his hearing. Parker said, "The kid from the hospital."

"He's going to come over to you," Liss said. "He's going to frisk you. Don't turn around."

Parker shrugged, with hands wide. Faint

movement behind him was reflected in the glass in front, not clear enough to be of any use. He said, "George, if you're holding a gun, put it away. I don't want to see it. We've got to get along if you're ever gonna see your share of the money."

"Are you carrying?"

"Yes."

"Here's my problem," Liss's slurring voice said. "Maybe I need you to get to the money. But if you know where it is, or where it's gonna be, why do you need me?"

That was the question. Parker had to finesse it and make it believable, or Liss would kill him here and now and try to figure out some other way to get to the money. The truth was, Parker needed Liss because Liss had a gun on him. Parker needed Liss only so long as Liss had the option to kill him. Parker needed Liss until they were back on an even footing. Then Parker would kill him.

Which was the thought he didn't want Liss to develop. He said, "George, ever since you made that little mistake with the shotgun, we've both been looking over our shoulder. I need my concentration for other things, and so do you. We don't have to kill each other, and we don't have to lose out on the money. We team up again, we start new. Just until we get the money. Then you go your way and I go mine, and you know I won't work with you again."

There was a long silence from behind him. Liss had to weigh it all, had to decide what was the likeliest thing to be the truth. But his judgment would be affected by the fact that he didn't know how to find the money and Parker did. That was why, at last, the slurring whispery voice said, "I never heard you were a forgiving guy."

"I'm not forgiving you, George. I know what a piece of shit you are. But I worked with a lot of guys over the years that I didn't want to see off the job. If I was only gonna work with gentlemen, I'd never work."

Liss laughed. "And isn't that the truth," he said. "All right, we'll try it your way for a while. But my partner's coming over there to take that gun off you. Or however many you have."

"Not needed, George."

"*I* need it, Parker," Liss said, and for the first time the strain was in his voice. "The other thing I could do, you know," the strained voice said, "I could gut-shoot you right now, and you'd still be able to lead me to the money later on but I wouldn't have to worry about you in between."

"And if I went into shock?"

"I'd chance it."

Liss might even do that, he was reckless enough. Parker didn't like giving up the gun he'd taken from Thorsen, but it was a risk he was going to have to accept. He said, "One gun, George, on my left side, above the waist."

"My partner's gonna pat you down."

Parker shrugged.

Silence. Shuffling sounds. Panting in Parker's ear, and a hand that snaked around his chest, feeling for the gun.

Parker saw a scenario. He takes out this one with an elbow, spins around behind him, fires at the spot where Liss's voice had been coming from.

But Liss would know that scenario himself. By now, he would have moved to one of the two corners of the room back there. Parker would be firing at an empty doorway, and Liss would have an angle on him that the punk's body wouldn't shield.

The hand found Thorsen's gun, tugged it out. The panting breath receded. Hands patted his shins, his pockets, like being touched by a flock of passing bats. The hands missed anywhere he might have had a second gun, and then they left.

Parker said, "George, when I turn around, I don't want to see your gun."

A little pause. "Fine," slurred the voice.

Parker turned, and the Quindero kid was in the open doorway to the next room, his face full of exhausted panic, Thorsen's gun dangling from his right hand, barrel pointed downward. In the left corner of the room, just by the head of that open staircase downward, Liss stood, watchful, waiting. His hands were empty.

5

One level down, there was more light because there was less plywood. This had originally been kitchen, dining room and maid's quarters, with bedrooms below that, and the owner's study at the bottom. With the conversion to the duplex, that fresh stairway had been cut in from the top floor to the maid's quarters, which then became the second bedroom of the upper apartment. The dining room down here became the living room of the lower apartment, with access via the original stairs, which were blocked off from the tenants up above.

The result was, this second level had been messed around with less. No new walls, no wholesale removal of windows. And, since below the top level access from without was very difficult on the ravine side, the windows down here had not been covered with plywood when the bank took over, and still showed the old view out over the ravine. From down here, in the original dining room, most of the development houses were invisible beyond the rim of the ravine, so you could look out and still see some of what had first attracted the site to the original owner and architect.

Squatters had lived in here from time to time. They'd pulled up the plywood that had been laid over the bathroom drains, so now you could use the space where the toilet had been as a toilet; but it was better to slide the plywood back over the hole when not in use. Some wooden boxes and old futons had been dragged down here by the onetime squatters as furniture. Nobody wanted to go near the futons, but the boxes made good chairs when placed against the wall.

Parker and Liss and the punk, Quindero, sat against three walls, Parker in the middle, facing the windows and the late afternoon view; sunlight on tumbled rocks and snarled woods, with the shadow of the building slowly creeping up the other side of the ravine. This place faced east, so the sunrise would look in on whoever was still here.

Liss sat to Parker's left, resting easy, legs out, back against the wall, hands in his lap with fingers curled upward. His eyes were hooded, and the active side of his face was almost as immobile as the frozen side. He was settled into a waiting mode, for as long as it took, patient, unmoving, a skill you learn on heists. Or in prison.

Ralph Quindero jittered to Parker's right. Nobody'd told him what to do with the little automatic, so it was on the floor between his feet, where his jittering made him bump into it with the sides of his shoes from time to time, each hit causing the automatic to scrape along the floor, each scrape sound making Quindero jump yet again. His hands twitched, moving from position to position, arms crossed, or hands resting on lap, or in pants pockets, or scratching his head and his arms and his knees. His eyes skittered back and forth, like a rodent, never looking at anything for long, bouncing every which way.

The stairway from above was just to Parker's left, a darker opening in this rear wall. The stairway down to the next level was along the right wall, between the windows and the jittering Quindero.

Did Liss count on this "partner" of his? Did he think Ralph Quindero would be any damn use at all? If not, why keep him around?

They didn't have much to talk about, but after a while Liss roused himself and said, "One thing."

Parker looked at him.

The good half of Liss's face smiled a little. He turned his head enough to look at Parker, and said, "What the hell were you doing in that hospital? You weren't after old Tom."

"No. Not the way you were. You saw the guy gave me a shove."

"Spoiled my aim."

"That's him. He's Archibald's security man."

Quindero, with his nervous whiny voice, unexpectedly joined the conversation: "I remember him."

They both ignored the interruption. Interested in what Parker had said, Liss raised the one eyebrow: "Oh, yeah?"

Pointing, Parker said, "That used to be his gun."

"He gave it to you?"

"Not exactly. I went back to the motel, looking for Mackey—"

"They won't go back there," Liss said, flat, with dismissive assurance.

"But they did," Parker told him. "Brenda and her cosmetics, remember?"

Liss didn't want to believe it. Gesturing at Quindero, he said, "With these wild cards in the deck? The motel was spoiled, we all knew that."

"Not later." Parker shrugged. "They went back, that's all, and checked out. That's why I know where they'll be at midnight. George, you can call the motel yourself. Jack Grant's still registered, but the Fawcetts are gone."

Liss thought that over, and decided he could believe Parker this time. "Hell," he said. "I could have had them. I'd never have thought it."

"While I was there," Parker said, "after Mackey and Brenda left and we made our arrangements, this guy Thorsen showed up, the security man. I told him I was an insurance investigator."

Liss gave a little snort. "You? Don't tell me he bought it."

"For a while."

"So the security guy's the one got you into the hospital. For the hell of it?"

"I wanted to talk to Carmody," Parker said, "only you got to him first."

"What the hell you want to talk to old Tom about?"

"You."

"What about me?"

"He was your parole guy. He might know people you knew, some way for me to track you down."

Liss looked confused and irritable. "Whadaya wanna track *me* down for? I didn't have the damn money."

"I wanted to kill you," Parker said.

Quindero jumped at that, the automatic

scraping on the floor, but Liss laughed. Then he nodded a while, thinking that over, and when he looked again at Parker he said, "You still want to kill me."

"Not necessarily," Parker told him. "Not if we all get our money. Your new partner here gets his out of yours, you know."

"Naturally," Liss said.

Liss and Parker looked at one another with faint smiles, both knowing how unlikely it was that anybody would share with anybody, and how impossible that Quindero would come out of this with anything at all. Anything at all.

Liss thought some more, then said, "You got any money on you?"

"A few bucks."

"There's a deli about half a mile from here. We can send Ralph out for some more food. Another pizza. And sodas. Unless you want beer."

Parker shook his head. As Liss knew, you didn't drink when you were working, and the both of them were working right now, very hard.

"Soda, then," Liss said. "You got a ten or a twenty?"

"You've got money, George."

"I'll pay my share," Liss assured him. "And Ralph's, too, the poor bastard doesn't have a dime on him, the cops took it all. And his ID, and his shoelaces, and everything. Isn't that right, Ralph?"

"Uh huh," Quindero said. He looked as though he suspected he was being made fun of, but knew better than to make an issue of it.

Parker took a twenty out of his wallet, and extended it toward Ralph, saying, "You come over here to get it. Then you go over to George to get his. Leave that gun right where it is."

Liss laughed. "You gonna make a dash for it?"

"No," Parker said.

Quindero looked at Liss, who told him, "Do it that way, Ralph, it's fine."

So Quindero got to his feet and came over to take Parker's twenty, then crossed to Liss, who said, "Lean down, Ralph, let me tell you especially what I want."

Liss whispered to Quindero, while Parker watched the shadows inch up the opposite side of the ravine. Then Quindero started for the door, and Parker told him, "George told you, call the motel, see did they really check out. Now, their name at the motel is Fawcett, be sure you get that right. And while you're at it, ask if Mr. Grant checked out, too." Looking at Liss, he said, "Because I didn't."

Liss laughed. "Shit, I was just hoping you'd lied to me. I mean, Parker, it's fine we're partners again and all that, but if it could turn out you don't know where that money is any more than I do, it would simplify my life, it really would."

Parker said to Quindero, "Be sure to make the call, and get the names right. George here is anxious to kill me, you know."

Quindero threw frightened looks at both of them. He stood in the doorway, clutching the money in his right hand.

Liss said, "Ralph. You know you'll come back."

"Yes," Quindero said.

"Because you got nowhere else to go," Liss told him. "I saved your ass, and I'll go on saving it. Just so long as you do what you're told."

Parker said, "Quindero. Have George describe his retirement plan some time."

Liss laughed, but then he said, "Parker, that isn't funny. Ralph is new at the game. Don't upset him."

Parker looked out at the ravine again, and Liss made shooing motions at Quindero, who scurried away.

They were silent for almost five minutes, sitting against two walls at right angles to one another, resting, not seeming to look at one another. Then Parker said, "What do you want him for, George? Besides to send for pizza."

"To throw out of the sled," Liss said.

6

It was unnatural to sit here like this. Parker needed Liss dead, and he knew Liss felt the same way about him, and they were both held back. Liss was held back because Parker was his only sure route to the duffel bags full of money, and Parker was held back because Liss had the gun.

After dark, Parker thought. A chance will come after dark.

The afternoon slowly descended outside, the sunny areas growing bright even as they narrowed, the shadows getting darker. The rock and the tangled underbrush out there would be full of creatures, wary, moving in sudden jumps, hidden away in the cat's cradle of vines and branches, living their lives with all senses alert. Darkness would be good for them, too.

Thorsen's gun was pale, standing out against the dark floor over next to the box where Quindero had been. Neither of them looked directly at it, but both knew it was there. Parker looked out the windows at the ravine and watched the light change. Liss didn't seem to look at anything.

Quindero was gone almost an hour, and when he came back he seemed more agitated than ever. He carried a brown paper shopping bag with handles, and when he came in he said, "My picture's in the paper."

They looked at him. Liss said, "Is it a good picture, Ralph? Is it one you like?"

Parker said, "Show me the paper." And held his hand out.

Quindero dithered, not sure what to do, looking first at Parker, then at Liss.

Liss did his half-grin. "You bought the paper, Ralph? Did you? For your scrapbook? Sure, go ahead, let Parker see it."

Quindero put the bag on the floor, rooted in it, came out with a newspaper, handed it to Parker. Then he carried the bag over to Liss, to divvy up the food.

It was this city's one newspaper, full-size, not tabloid. It was heavy on the ads, heavy on the wire service reports, with just barely enough local staff to cover robbery, murder, arson and escapes all happening at once. Under the main headline:

WITNESS MURDERED IN
MEMORIAL HOSPITAL
Police Guard
Not Enough;
Killer Escapes

was an excited story about the events in the hospital, plus a recap of the robbery at the stadium, plus a lot of self-confident official pronouncements.

Three photos of equal size and importance ran horizontally under the main headline and next to the subhead and story. From left to right, they were the local police commissioner, Tom Carmody and Ralph Quindero. The newspaper couldn't have done a better job of taking attention away from Ralph Quindero's features if they'd decided not to run the picture at all.

The photo they'd used of Quindero was a black-and-white blowup of something from the family's collection, and it showed him in sunshine, full face, smiling and squinting, two things he wasn't likely to do for a while. When Parker looked at this picture and its placement, and then looked at Ralph Quindero, it seemed to him Quindero could probably walk through the newspaper's editorial department without anybody recognizing him.

Over next to Liss, Quindero squatted down and ripped up the paper bag into large irregular pieces to use as plates. On one of these, he brought Parker two slices of pizza, plus a can of some local bottler's cola. A bottle would have been more useful, but it didn't matter.

It was getting darker in here, hard to read, but once everybody was settled, with Quindero once again seated against the right wall, mouth full of pizza, Parker held the newspaper angled to catch the light from the windows and out loud read, "Walter Malloy, the Quindero family attorney, issued a plea late this morning for fugitive Ralph Quindero to give himself up, saying, 'There are no substantive charges against Ralph. At this point, the police merely want to talk to him as a witness. The longer he stays in hiding, the more he risks facing some sort of charge down the line.' Police have announced a special telephone number for anyone with information on any aspect of the investigation." Parker looked over at Quindero: "You want the number?"

Quindero blinked a lot, staring back and forth between Parker and Liss. "What does that— What do they *mean?*"

Parker said, "Oley oley in free."

Liss laughed, and looked at Quindero, and

told him, "It's a good thing we don't believe what we read in the newspapers, huh, Ralph?"

Quindero simply stared at him.

"Because, if you *did* believe that bullshit," Liss went on, "I'd have to kill you now. I can't have you go home and tell stories about me. But we don't believe it, so that's okay."

Quindero said, "We don't believe it?"

"Oh, come on, Ralph," Liss said. "That's the stuff they say every time. They'd say it to *me* if they could. Come on in, there's no problem, nobody's mad at you. Oh, okay, you say, I'm all right. And you go in, and the first thing, they slap the cuffs on you. You've had the cuffs on you, remember, Ralph?"

"I remember," Quindero said.

"And that was *before* all this other stuff. Everything's okay and you should come in *now*? When back before old Tom got his, and you and I headed out of there, way back *then* they had the cuffs on you?"

"That's right," Quindero said.

Liss looked at Parker, and shook his head. "Parker, why do you want to upset my partner here? That's not a good thing to do."

Parker looked at the top of the paper. "It says there's a chance of rain tomorrow."

"We don't care about that," Liss said. "We're long gone by then. One way or another."

7

I t's getting too dark in here," Liss said.

They'd all been silent for a long while, Quindero brooding, Liss and Parker both waiting. But it was true; darkness had spread in this east-facing room, faster than outside, where the shadow across the way had not yet quite reached the rim of the ravine. Clear sunshine tinged with red made a kind of fire along the rim, a line of concentrated brightness, with the sky beyond it a deep blue turning gray. Inside, they could still see one another, but no one would be able to read the newspaper. Thorsen's gun no longer gleamed on the floor. And Liss wasn't happy.

Parker felt Liss's eyes on him, but didn't respond. He kept on watching the rim of the ravine out there. When the last of the sunshine left, there would be a sudden drop in reflected light into this room. Not a big change, not even very noticeable. But enough to make everything blur, everything out of focus, until their eyes could adjust. In that instant, Parker would go for Thorsen's gun.

But Liss was unhappy. "Parker," he said, "I don't know about this."

"What's the problem, George?"

"Same as always. You."

Parker kept watching the rim. The sun moved very slowly. "Nothing's changed," he said. "We're all still like we were."

"I don't want you loose when it's dark in here," Liss said.

"Midnight doesn't come for a while, George."

"Even if I had a flashlight, I couldn't use it," Liss said. "Not with all those windows. There's always some nosy son of a bitch with time on his hands to call the cops."

"We've been doing fine up till now, George." The light hung on the rim, golden red. The air was so clear you could see individual branches, fall shades of yellow and tan on the weeds and underbrush, turned Technicolor by the sun.

Liss abruptly stood. "Ralph," he said, "put your foot on that gun."

Parker didn't bother to watch Quindero obey. He also stood, watching Liss's hands, waiting for one of them to reach to a pocket or behind his back. "George," he said, "don't fuck things up."

"There's a closet," Liss said. "Ralph and me, we looked the place over when we first got here. Downstairs, next story down, there's a closet with a door on it and a lock on the outside."

"George, you don't want me to—"

"It's that or I wound you," Liss said. The strain was coming back into his voice. "Maybe that'd be easier anyway. Don't have to gut-shoot you, I can take out both your knees, and Ralph can carry you when it's time to go."

Quindero made a little startled sound, not quite a protest.

Parker said, "Better have Ralph test that first. See how far he can carry me."

Quindero stammered and said, "I don't— I don't think I could do that." He was a reedy weedy thing, a poor specimen.

Liss had to know it, but he also had to protect himself. "Goddamit, Parker," he said. "I want you out of the way, locked up, where I don't have to worry about you all the time. Eleven-thirty, we'll let you out, we'll all get out of here. Meantime, Ralph and me, we'll go get a car."

"George—"

"We do it my way!"

Parker was silent, thinking. A closet till eleven-thirty? Half an hour after Brenda and Mackey

248

would drive by the motel, and they surely wouldn't wait. But could a closet hold him that long? Liss and Quindero had to go get a car. He said, "Make it eleven. It could take a while to get there."

"Eleven," Liss agreed. "But I can't have you out here, Parker, you understand that. I'll have to shoot you, either to kill or wound. I can't have you around."

"I'll wait, George," Parker said. "Where is this closet of yours?"

"Downstairs. Next flight down. You lead the way."

The light hung on the rim of the ravine. Parker shrugged and turned toward the stairs. Behind him, Liss said, "Ralph, bring along that fucking gun."

8

It was darker down here, with all these interior walls separating off bedrooms and bathrooms, but Liss and Quindero were behind him, keeping their distance, and there was no advantage to be made of the darkness. Parker went down the stairs, and at the bottom, from behind him, Liss said, "Around to the right," which was the hall through the middle of the building.

Parker saw that the closet Liss was talking about was the one that used to be the elevator shaft. The lock was a hasp, with a wooden dowel stuck in it. Liss, still keeping well back, said, "Take the dowel out. Hand it back to Ralph."

Parker did that, and opened the door, and only a faint odor of dry wood came out. It was black inside there, impossible to see a thing.

Liss, sounding more and more nervous, said, "What's the problem? Get in there."

It wouldn't do to have Liss lose control; he was the one with the guns. Parker said, "Take it easy, George. It's dark in here, I gotta feel my way."

He took a step forward, reaching his arms out, and at first encountered nothing. The elevator, when it had been in place, had been deeper than wide, comfortable for two people, possible for three if they knew one another. Now that the space was a closet, the front half was empty, but when Parker stepped in deeper, his hands met the round horizontal wooden pole toward the back for hanging clothes on, and the wooden shelf above it. Both were empty, and so was the floor.

The pole and shelf were at head height, but there was plenty of room in front of them. Parker turned around to look out at Liss and Quindero, in the hall with the staircase behind them. "All right, George," he said. "Go get your car."

Liss said to Quindero, "Shut it. Put the dowel in. Make sure it's goddam tight."

Quindero came forward. His eyes met Parker's just before he shut the door, and they were full of panic. But he'd go on obeying Liss, because there wasn't one solitary other thing he could think of to do.

The door closed. In absolute darkness, he heard the dowel scrape into place. Then it sounded as though Quindero was pounding the dowel in tighter, probably with the butt of Thorsen's gun. Shoot his own elbow off, if he wasn't careful.

Late for Ralph Quindero to be careful.

Parker went down on the floor, pressing his cheek to the plywood floor and his head against the base of the door, his ear next to the space under the door. He heard Quindero back away, heard him say, "It's good and tight."

"Good."

"Do we go get the car now?"

"No. When it's dark. Come on upstairs."

The steps went away. Two pairs, receding down the hall, then mounting the stairs.

Parker sat up, rested his back against the plywood wall, and crossed his forearms on his knees. His watch didn't glow in the dark, which was sometimes an advantage and sometimes not.

It didn't matter. He was better in here for now, not making Liss antsy. There was plenty of time to come out.

9

It was probably time. Parker had listened now and then at that space at the bottom of the door, but heard nothing, so Liss and Quindero weren't bothering to check on him in here. He'd seen the faint gray line of light under the door shadow and blur, until at last it disappeared into the general black. He'd gone on waiting, and now it was probably time to get out of here.

Did Liss understand what these closets were? Maybe not. They were afterthoughts, simple structures inserted to make use of the space. These closets were not structural, and therefore had none of the building's support beams going through their ceilings and floors. Simple stringers, two-by-six lengths of wood, had been toed into place to support plywood floors; that was it. And Ed Mackey had already showed them how to lift the floor in the bottom-level closet, to find the motor well for use as a hiding place for the duffel bags.

Parker went down on all fours and started in a front corner, patting the floor, looking for a seam. He found it where he expected it to be, about a foot and a half back from the doorway opening, the same place it had been downstairs. When they'd added these closets, they'd laid one sheet of plywood from the rear of the space to near the front, to give themselves leeway in fitting the piece in, and then they'd cut a second piece to fill the remaining space.

Next, he stood and felt his way to the back of the closet, where he patted the underpart of the shelf until he came to one of the two L-shaped brackets that the shelf rested on. It would have been easier if the shelf had just been placed there, but they'd screwed it to the brackets, so he stood under the shelf, bent down, kept out of the way of the wooden clothes pole, and punched upward with the heels of both hands, flanking one of the brackets, until the shelf broke loose.

When the shelf popped upward, with a quick ripping sound, one of the screws fell out and bounced on the floor. Parker paused, listening for a reaction. There'd been very little noise, but he couldn't be sure they hadn't heard it. If they were in the building.

After three or four minutes, when he still heard nothing, he went back to work, holding the shelf up out of the way with one hand while twisting the bracket back and forth with the other, until the screws holding it to the wall came loose. This part he managed to do with almost no noise at all.

Now he had the bracket for a tool. It was three inches along one side and four inches along the other, thin but strong metal. He put this to work on the floor, gouging along the seam line until he'd torn a slit wide enough to squeeze the bracket into. Kneeling on the larger section of floor, bearing down on the bracket, he pried the smaller section up one fraction at a time. Four screws had been drilled down into the corners of this piece, plus one each at front and back into the central stringer. It was the rear screw in the stringer that Parker pried out first, then the left corner, then the right. Then he could peel this piece up and back toward the door, until the other three screws gave way.

Now he had a space a foot and a half by five feet, with a two-by-six stringer across the middle and Sheetrock underneath. Using the bracket, Parker sliced through the Sheetrock a piece at a time, breaking the pieces off to bring them up into the closet and lay on the floor here, not wanting pieces of ceiling to fall and make a racket.

When he made the first hole in the Sheetrock, he saw gray light again, very dim, defining the jagged hole. There was no door on the ground floor closet, and whatever light was coming in the study windows reached back to here.

Parker removed chunks of ceiling, clearing the space, then slid down through the opening feet first. He had to wriggle his torso through the narrow opening, had to hold his arms over his head and at last just permit himself to drop.

He landed with knees bent, and let himself fall forward, hands hitting the floor, elbows flexing, allowing his body to drop to the left, until his shoulder hit the side wall of the closet. He stayed in that position, awkward, crouched on hands and knees, bent body leaning leftward, shoulder against wall, back to the open doorway. He listened, and waited, and heard nothing.

In silence, he shifted away from the wall. He put his left hand on the wall, and straightened. On his feet, he turned to look out across the stripped study at the angled row of windows, and they were bathed in blue-gray light. He moved toward them. There was stiffness to be worked out of his system, so as he crossed the study he moved his arms and shoulders, limbering up, feeling the sore points.

A half moon had risen above the ravine, and now looked down toward this side of the house. The newspaper had said it might rain by tomorrow, and there was just a hint of haze over the moon, but for right now it gave plenty of light. Maybe too much. Later it would climb above the house and give almost no light to the interior. And if the clouds came in, there'd be nothing but darkness inside here.

Parker moved slowly through the house, up through the levels, carrying the L bracket, his only weapon and tool. He searched the rooms as he went through, but they'd all been stripped, there was nothing left he could use.

And there was nobody here. The moonlight let him see his watch, and the time was nine-twenty. So Liss and Quindero must be out picking up a car. Parker needed them to come back soon, so he could finish this in time to meet Brenda and Mackey.

The dining room, where they'd waited out the afternoon, was very bright, being closer to the top of the ravine and with all those large windows facing right at the moon. Quindero had left his newspaper on the floor near the box where he'd been sitting, and the light was bright enough to read the headlines. If you held the paper close to a window and squinted, you could probably read everything in it, but there was nothing in there Parker needed to know.

He went on up to the top floor, and crossed to the spot in the rear corner where you could look out through the plywood sheathing at the road and the fence. The fence now gleamed silver, reflecting the moonlight, to make everything behind it a fuzzy blurry black.

Parker leaned against the wall and watched the road. He had come here to this house in the first place only because there were too many people in this town looking for him. He'd needed somewhere to lie low until it was time to go meet Brenda and Mackey, and this was the best place he knew. Finding Liss here had been an extra gift, a way to close the books on this job entirely, but if it wasn't going to work out it wasn't going to work out.

If Liss and Quindero didn't come back by ten, he'd have to leave, forget about them. Go meet with Brenda and Mackey, if they were there, and worry about dealing with Liss later.

Ten o'clock. Half an hour from now. Working the stiffness out of his shoulders and arms, Parker waited.

10

Nine-fifty. Light, moving through the woods.

Is he driving the car in here? Over *that* road?

But maybe it made sense. The road was almost nonexistent, but Liss might be more comfortable driving on it than having to walk back to the main road in total darkness. Particularly with Parker at his side.

Yes, here it came, very slowly. Some sort of four-door sedan. Liss drove with parking lights only, just enough amber illumination out front to give him a sense of where the road was. Now he swung the car to the left, just the other side of the fence, reversed, swung forward again, and backed up almost to the fence, facing out. Making it easier for himself for the return.

Liss hadn't removed the interior light. It

flashed on as they got out of the car, and Parker saw that Liss had been driving and his new partner was still alive.

Parker moved into the shadows away from where they would enter the house. He could hear them talking as they neared it, and when they came through the break in the plywood he could make out the words. Liss was saying "—trust him. He doesn't trust me, and he's right, and I don't trust him, and I'm right. If he can take us down, he will. Ralph, you listening?"

"Yes." The voice was small, quavery, frightened, but determined.

"We gotta work together," Liss said, "or he'll kill us both. You hear what I'm saying?"

"Why don't we just leave him?" Quindero asked. "Just walk away now and take the car and get away from here and just *leave* him down there."

"I need the money," Liss said. "*We* need the money, Ralph, you and me. Your half is two hundred grand, just keep thinking about that. You need that money, if you're gonna get to Canada, start over."

So that's the fairy tale they're telling each other. Parker followed, well behind, as they went downstairs toward the dining room.

Liss said, "We gotta keep him with us, and we gotta keep him alive, until we see if he really does know where the money is. Then we can deal with him. But before then, we gotta keep *him* from doing *us*. Jesus, it's bright in here."

They were in the dining room now, Parker on the stairs behind them.

Quindero said, "That's good, isn't it? If there's light, we can see him."

"Here's what we're going to do," Liss said. "I'll wait here. You go down and— Wait. Where's that gun of his?"

"Here."

"Give it to me," Liss said. "I don't want him taking it off you."

"You want me to go down there without a gun? Where are *you* going to be?"

"Up here."

"But—"

"Just listen," Liss said, and Parker sat down on the stairs to listen. Liss said, "You go down there and take that piece of wood out of the lock. Do it quiet if you can. Then get back into some dark corner somewhere that he's not gonna see you, and then shout to him to come out. Then *I'll* shout from up here, and I'll tell him to come up. Then he'll come up and you'll come up behind him."

"So he's in between us."

"That's right," Liss said.

Quindero said, "But if I don't have a gun? What good is it if—"

"Does *he* know that? What if he sees you, and instead of coming upstairs he makes a jump for you? If you've got a gun, you're not gonna use it. So you show him your hands, you tell him you don't have any weapons on you, they're all up with me. He knows he has to come up past me before he can get out. And I'll call to him, I'll say, 'Don't mess with my partner, I'm up here, come up.' And he'll come up."

Liss was explaining all this as though Quindero was a six-year-old, and he was probably right to play it that way. Another professional would already know most of what Liss was saying, but Ralph Quindero was not a professional.

And now Quindero said, "Okay, he comes up here. And then what?"

"I'll move ahead of him," Liss said. "I'll go up those stairs over there, ahead of him, and we'll tell him to follow, and you come along behind. And we'll go out to the car that way, me always in front of him, you always behind him, so he can never get the both of us."

"What if he jumps you?"

"I'll put one in his arm," Liss said. "It'll stop him, but it won't kill him, and it won't put him into shock. Maybe I ought to do that anyway."

Quindero said, "Don't," pleading.

Liss was amused. "What, you don't like loud noises? Or is it blood you're afraid of?"

"We don't have to shoot him," Quindero said. Now he sounded sullen.

Liss said, "Haven't you been listening? Of *course* we have to shoot him, sooner or later. We have to shoot him dead. When we get there, wherever the money's supposed to be, we're gonna shoot him then."

"Why? Why do we have to?"

"You want him behind you, the rest of your life?"

Quindero didn't say anything to that. They were shuffling around down there in the dining room, doing something Parker couldn't see, because he didn't want to descend the stairs far enough that he might be noticed, and then Liss said, "Okay, go on down and let him out."

Parker rose, silent, as he heard Quindero thump down the next flight of stairs. He eased downward, step by step, until he could see into the room, bluish gray in the moonlight, the boxes and trash throwing long black shadows across the gray floor. He looked left and right, and at first he didn't see Liss at all. Where was he?

Oh. Smart. Liss was seated on the floor directly under the windows, in the middle of that long wall. It was the one place in the room where he'd be hard to see, and he'd stay there until he was sure things were going right with Quindero.

But things wouldn't go right with Quindero. And where Liss had placed himself, Parker couldn't get at him. He'd never get across that large room without being seen, and shot.

"Hey! Mr. Parker! Come on out!"

Parker eased back up the stairs. He'd have to come at them in some other way.

It was too late now to get away from here. If he took the car, he wouldn't be able to drive it at better than a walking pace between here and the main road. Liss would have no trouble catching up. If he went on foot, Liss could get close enough to him with the car's headlights to bring him down.

He had to stay here, and finish it.

11

When the house had been divided into two, the main staircase had been segregated from the top floor area by a new wall, but when the failed attempt had been made to restore the place to its original condition that extra wall had been removed, which meant Parker could now come up to the top floor, go to his left, and in the far corner find the additional set of stairs that had been added to give access to what had originally been the maid's quarters.

As he moved, he could hear them shouting back and forth:

"He's not coming out! He isn't coming out!"

"Ralph! Go over and open the door!"

"I don't want to!"

"Shit. Parker! Ralph doesn't have the gun, I do! Come on out of there!"

Construction materials were still scattered around, particularly up here where the duplex had been made and then unmade. Parker had earlier noticed a few scraps of plywood and other junk along the partition where the second staircase had been cut in, and now, while Liss and Quindero went on shouting at one another, he felt around in that rubbish, and came up with a stub of two-by-four about two feet long. He hefted it, and it wasn't very heavy, but it was the best he could find.

Carrying the two-by-four in his right hand and the L bracket in his left, he went quietly down the new stairs into the maid's quarters, and from there into the original kitchen. He was now one room away from Liss, who was yelling, "Ralph! Dammit, open the door!"

Silence. Parker edged around the doorway between kitchen and dining room, and Liss hadn't moved, except to go up on one knee. But he was still in the same place, against the windows, unreachable.

"He isn't here! Jesus, I almost fell! There's a *hole* in the floor!"

"Parker!" Liss shouted, looking from doorway to doorway. "Parker, dammit!"

"He's gone!"

"Ralph! Come up out of there!"

But still Liss wouldn't move away from that safe position against the outer wall. Parker could see his head framed against the window, now that he was up on one knee. He was turning left and right, watching everything. He was going to be hard to get at.

Watching him, Parker considered. What if he were to come out now, show himself to Liss, go back to the idea that they were all traveling together?

No. Not any more. Liss was too spooked by now. He *would* put a bullet into Parker, just to slow him down.

Quindero came clattering up the stairs. When he appeared, Liss at last got to his feet, still wary. Quindero hurried across to him, crying, "He got away! He's gone!"

Quietly, Liss said, "He's here."

Quindero, bewildered, looked around at the moonlit room. "What? But he escaped."

"He's in the house," Liss said, "waiting his shot at us."

"What are we going to do?"

"Pull those rags and shit into the middle of the room," Liss told him. "What we need is more light."

"You mean a fire?"

"Then we go upstairs and wait. When he gets hot enough, he'll come up and visit."

Parker watched them shift the trash to a low mound in the middle of the room. Liss used Quindero's newspaper to start the fire, then stood over it until a few rags and some scraps of wood also caught. Then, looking around, he called, "Parker! Whatever you got in mind, it isn't gonna work. Come on out."

Voice hushed, Quindero said, "He must have heard us before, what we were talking. What we were gonna do."

"Shut up, Ralph," Liss said, almost absent-mindedly. "We didn't say anything he didn't already know." He now had his own pistol in his right hand, Thorsen's automatic in his left. "Okay, it's burning," he said. "Time to go upstairs. You watch for him, in case he comes up over there. Let me get about halfway, and then follow me."

"All right."

Parker waited in the kitchen doorway, as Liss started up the stairs to the top floor, going almost immediately out of sight. Quindero stood staring at the stairs from below until Liss called down to him, "Come on, Ralph."

"I don't see him," Quindero said.

"You will," Liss said. "Come on up."

The instant Quindero turned toward the

upper staircase, Parker came out from the kitchen. Moving fast, two-by-four cocked over his shoulder, he crossed the dining room, firelight throwing his shadows around the walls, and reached the staircase when Quindero was only up to the third step.

Liss yelled, "Ralph! Down!"

But Quindero was too slow. He didn't drop, the way Liss wanted, but spun around, open-mouthed, so the two-by-four, instead of hitting him in the back of the head, smacked into his left ear and cheek.

Liss fired anyway, and the slug punched into Quindero's right shoulder blade, spinning him farther around. Dazed, stunned, Quindero would have fallen, but Parker grabbed him with his left arm and held him as a shield, the way Liss had done in the hospital. The difference was, Liss didn't care about shields. He fired three more times, trying to hit Parker around Quindero or through him, he didn't care which.

Parker felt the impacts in Quindero's body, felt him go limp. His hand that held the L bracket pressed Quindero tight to him, and he backed hurriedly away from the stairs, dragging the body. In the middle of the room, he tossed Quindero across the small fire, hoping to smother it, or at least cut down on all that light.

Liss would come down, so Parker had to go

up. Below here, there was only the one staircase, and he'd be trapped. On the top floor, where the glass was covered by plywood all around, there was almost no light. A two-by-four and an L bracket and darkness, that was what he had. Liss had two guns.

12

Parker eased off the stairs into the darkness of the top floor. He stopped, and listened, and heard nothing. Liss must be doing the same thing. But where? Had he gone down where the light is, to be safe? Or was he still up here?

He waited, hand against the partition wall, trying to see shapes in the dark. Ahead of him, where the main stairs would be, there was no light at all, but faint gray lines of light were visible at the periphery, where sheets of plywood didn't quite meet.

Very slowly, Parker moved to his right, along the partition wall. He meant to circle around until he was the other side of the main stairs. Then he could look down and see if Liss was framed against the light down there.

Two quick shots, in this room, echoing in the big open empty space. Then a third, from a different gun, that bit into the wall just to his left. In the flashes, Parker got an afterimage of Liss, at the head of the stairs, firing both guns. Then he realized what Liss was doing. He was firing his pistol just for the flashes of light, shooting it anywhere, not aiming at anything in particular, and then firing Thorsen's automatic at Parker when he had him fixed.

Parker crouched and hurried along the wall, and now there were two shots, one from each gun, and he heard one bullet whack into the wall above his head. Liss was closing with him. It was a good system, it was going to work, Liss firing one gun for the light, the other for the kill.

Parker stopped, stepped back the other way, and threw the two-by-four at the spot where the flashes had been. Then he ran forward, hearing Liss yell when the two-by-four hit, following that sound, seeing the flash very close when Liss fired again to use the light. The afterimage of Liss's staring face was with him as he launched himself low, under the second shot, and crashed into Liss's legs.

They went down in a tumble, Parker grabbing for anything he could find, Liss swinging with the gun in his right hand, Parker chopping with the L bracket. Liss screamed, and a gun went skittering away across the floor. Parker chopped and chopped with the L bracket, climbing up Liss as though he were a steep hill. Liss shrieked again, and kicked out, desperately, and rolled free.

Parker sat up and heard Liss tumble down the stairs. He went over onto hands and knees and scrambled to the head of the stairs, and saw the bulky shape of Liss crawl away across the dining room down there.

The fire on the floor was out, though from the smell it must have burned a little of Quindero before it died.

Parker sat still, trying to remember. He'd heard the rattle of one of the guns, spinning away across the floor. Which way? Not down the stairs. Left? Yes; over there, to the left.

He crawled in that direction, patting the floor. There was silence from below, but Liss wasn't done, not yet. Where was the gun? Where was it? Where was it?

Here. Parker touched it, picked it up. It was Thorsen's automatic. How many rounds were left in it? Three or four at most.

He'd hurt Liss, he knew that, but didn't know how badly he was wounded. Was Liss still agile? Was he coming up the other stairs, or had he retreated to that position under the windows again? Or would he try to restart the fire?

Parker went on hands and knees back to the head of the stairs. He heard scuffling sounds from down below, but couldn't see Liss. He slid forward, and went slowly down the stairs head first, keeping his descent under control with his elbows on the steps. At the bottom, he looked over at the windows, but Liss wasn't there. He looked the other way, still saw nothing, and slid from the stairs down to the floor.

He had just started to rise, getting hands and knees under himself again, when Liss's head and arm and pistol appeared just above the stairs down to the next level. He'd been standing down there, just out of sight. He fired one shot, but Parker had dropped back to the floor when he heard the first sound of Liss's movement. The bullet hit the wall behind him, and lying there he twisted around to fire at Liss's retreating face, but missed.

He rolled away to his left, came upright, and Liss popped up again, aiming, firing.

They both heard the click.

Liss made a small strangled sound and dropped out of sight. Parker got to his feet and ran across the room and could just make out Liss's retreating shape at the foot of the stairs. He fired, but didn't hit anything, and Liss scurried away.

Parker went rapidly down the stairs. This level

was the little maze of bedrooms and bathrooms, and the closet where they'd held him for a while. Standing at the foot of the stairs, Thorsen's automatic in his hand, he listened. Sooner or later, he'd have to hear Liss's breathing.

"Parker."

Liss was off to the right, sounding as though he'd taken cover inside one of the rooms off this central hall. Parker turned in that direction, and waited.

"Parker, I'm hurt."

Parker moved two quick quiet steps forward while Liss spoke, then stopped.

"I just want out of here. Parker? Take the car, do what you want. Call it quits. We can only mess each other up even more. Call it off."

Parker moved when Liss spoke, stopped when he was silent. He'd reached the doorway now. Liss would be in the darkness just inside this room.

"Parker, why should we—? You son of a bitch, you're right *here*!"

There must have been some light behind Parker, that he'd now blocked with his body. Liss suddenly leaped at him, punching, kicking, trying to get past him. Parker pushed him off, to get a good shot, but Liss bounded away into the hall, and Parker fired after him, at all the noise he was making.

They both heard the click.

Silence. Parker reversed the automatic, gripping it by the barrel. What would Liss do now?

"Parker? Parker, listen, we're done, we're both done. Quit it. Neither of us has anything any more. Forget it, it's over."

Parker had moved forward while Liss talked, and now he swung the butt of the automatic at the spot where the voice had come from. He hit something, something solid that recoiled away. Liss yelled and retreated, and suddenly he went thundering down the final flight of stairs, down to the first owner's study.

Parker stood at the head of the stairs, listening to Liss gasp and curse down there. Bottom of the house. No way out.

Time to go down there and end it.

13

The moon was higher now, and only one narrow band of its light reached into the study, a stripe of silver-gray along the floor next to the windows. In that stripe Liss stood, panting, hunched, his right arm across his torso, protecting wounds.

Parker came down the stairs and stopped, still in darkness. Liss couldn't see him, but he looked across to where he knew Parker must be, and said, "I'm all done, Parker. Leave me here."

"I'm going to," Parker said, and moved toward him.

Liss waved his left hand back and forth, as though to stop him. His breath was heavier and more ragged, his body hunched in tighter. "Let it go!" he cried. "You'll get the money, you'll get everything. Let it go."

"If I leave you here," Parker said, "you'll rat me out, for a plea bargain."

"Then take me along. Not to the money, just to get away from here."

"I don't need you," Parker said, and reached for him, and Liss came around hard with the knife he'd been concealing under his right hand and arm, pressed to his torso. A switchblade, with four inches of knife.

Parker jumped back, and the knife sliced shirt and skin just under his heart, scraping on bone. Parker kicked Liss's knee, but then had to retreat again as Liss swung the knife once more.

Parker still held the automatic by the barrel, but it wouldn't be any good as a club against that knife. He'd have to be in too close, and Liss could cut him up from farther out.

They moved in little jerks and pauses, back into the darkness, away from the band of light beneath the windows. The knife was a faint gleam, moving like a dowsing rod in Liss's hand, dowsing for blood.

Parker paused, and Liss lunged. Parker chopped the butt of the automatic at Liss's wrist, but only hit it a glancing blow, and then had to skip backward again.

They circled one another in the large room,

slowly, with sudden dashes by Liss, trying to get that knife in among Parker's ribs. Parker dodged a dozen lunges, but Liss cut him twice more, and then again.

Parker's back was to the windows. There was nothing useful down here, no trash on the floor, nothing he could turn into a weapon. And Liss was crowding him closer, trying to get him into the corner of the room, the windows to his right, the solid wall to his left.

He couldn't let that happen, he couldn't let Liss corner him. He was still a few feet from the windows, there was still time. He feinted left, and then right, and then threw the automatic at Liss's head. He jumped in when Liss ducked, grabbed a double handful of shirtfront, and then rolled himself backward down onto the floor. His feet went up as he went down and back, his ankles catching Liss in the groin, lifting him up, the double grip on his shirtfront pulling him inexorably up and over, Liss swinging desperately back and forth with the knife, slicing Parker's forearms as Parker heaved him up into the air and over in a midair somersault, and through the window behind him with a great shout of smashing glass.

Parker rolled quickly away from descending dishes of jagged glass. A scream rolled back into the window from the cool outer air, cut short.

Parker sat up. His chest and forearms stung where the knife had drawn its lines, and his body was sore all over, but he had no serious wounds. The dizziness he felt right now would soon pass.

Leaning forward, he put his watch into the moonlight, and forced his eyes to focus. Almost quarter past ten. Just time enough to make the meet with Brenda and Mackey.

Slowly he got to his feet, and looked around, at the ruined house and the gaping hole in the window. Then he went up the stairs.

CLICK

I'm getting bored," Brenda said.

Ed kept on looking at the TV: CNN, multi-vehicle collision in fog on an interstate in California, blonde-haired woman solemn over her mike with ambulances in the background. He was waiting for the TV to tell him something new about events in this town right here, far from California and its fog. Outside this motel room, halfway around town from their first motel, the late afternoon sky was clear, visibility perfect. Inside, nobody on television, not local or network or cable, wanted to tell him what was happening *here*.

Brenda said, "Ed? When are we getting out of here?"

"Late tonight," Ed told her, pretending to be patient. "You know why. You saw the TV."

"California," she said, and gave the television set a look of scorn.

"Come on, Brenda. Before."

She knew, of course, he meant the business about Liss shooting up the local hospital, then taking off with some goon called Quindero that the cops wanted back unharmed for some reason. The law had been irritated already with just the robbery, but then you throw in Liss killing a guy the cops have under guard, right in front of them, and you could expect the locals were truly itching by now to get their hands on somebody. Anybody at all.

Which was the point Ed wanted to make. "They're all over this town like a bad smell," he said. "We did enough running around here today. When it turns dark, I get us a nice little car, not flashy, nothing you look at twice, and *then* we clear out of here."

They'd each been out of this room once since they'd checked in at this motel, Ed paying cash and using a driver's license for ID that had no history on it at all. First Ed had taken the most recent borrowed car back to the parking garage, to make their trail loop back on itself, and then he'd walked from there to a luggage store, where he'd bought three suitcases from a matched set and cabbed them back here, so they'd no longer be people with duffel bags. And then, a little after noon, Brenda had said, "The hell with it, I want my stuff," and over Ed's objections she'd cabbed back across town to their old motel.

She hadn't been completely careless, not at all. She'd left the cab two blocks from the motel, walked around the area, studied it, was very patient, and only when she was sure nobody had the place staked out did she go boldly back to their old room, where she packed up all her goods plus Ed's shaving kit and change of underwear. On her way out she noticed the woman in the office eyeballing her, so she went over there and checked out. "The people in the room next to you," the woman said, half-whispering, afraid the cockroaches might hear and pass it on, "they had something to do with that big robbery."

Brenda widened her eyes. "They did?"

"Might have killed us all in our sleep," the woman said.

"That's not much of a recommendation for your motel," Brenda pointed out.

The woman lowered her eyebrows and hunched down over her counter. "You can't be too careful," she said.

"Words to live by," Brenda agreed, and took another cab back to the new motel, where Ed hadn't moved, and CNN was showing distant explosions on a green mountainside. "Piece of cake," she said.

Ed kept his eyes on the screen. "Everybody else," he said, "has a woman constantly nagging: 'Be careful, be careful.' I got a woman, *I'm* the one says be careful."

"I was careful," Brenda assured him. "I didn't want you to see *me* on that TV."

"Be nice to see something, though," Ed said.

They saw something, at six o'clock, on the local news. They saw ambulances and stretchers and hundreds of official people, all in front of some big hotel downtown, behind an excited reporter yelling into his microphone about how one of the stadium robbers had posed as an insurance investigator until Reverend William Archibald's head of security unmasked him, when the robber damaged a whole lot of people and escaped. "Huh," Ed said. "Parker's a woolly guy."

"And all I did," Brenda reminded him, "was go back to the motel."

"Well, Parker's far from here by now, anyway," Ed suggested.

"And I wish I was," Brenda told him.

"Patience. Later. Patience."

* * *

COMEBACK

The guy in the motel office had said there was a good Italian restaurant two blocks down to the left, so that's where they'd go, around eight o'clock, and pick up a car on the way back, and be on the road by ten. At quarter to eight, Brenda went into the bathroom to freshen up her makeup for the journey to the restaurant, and two minutes later she came out with a scrunched-up expression on her face and an open compact in her left palm. "Ed," she said. "Take a look at this."

He looked. "It's dirty," he said. "The mirror's all streaked."

"It's a message. Come here in the light."

So he went back into the bathroom with her, where the light was brighter, and she said, "Eleven P.M. See it?"

"Shit," Ed said.

"He wants us to pick him up."

Ed looked shifty. She could tell he didn't like this idea. "He doesn't say where."

"Come on, Ed. Back at the motel."

"Not a chance," Ed decided. "You ready? Let's go eat."

They fought about it through dinner, leaning toward one another over their plates, Brenda hissing while Ed muttered. The waiters thought it was a lovers' quarrel, and gave them space.

Ed had all the arguments, and all Brenda had was persistence. He said, "We don't know who wrote that, even. It could have been George, and we walk right back into shit."

"It's Parker, and you know it," Brenda said. "And he expects us."

"If it was the other way around, he wouldn't come back for me, you can bet on it. And I wouldn't expect it."

"It isn't the other way around," Brenda said. "You aren't him, you're you, and he knows we'll come back for him."

"Then it's *you* he's counting on, not me."

Brenda shrugged. "Okay."

"Brenda, he's got the whole fucking *state* looking for him, they've probably even got him by now. *And,* if they pick him up anywhere near that motel, they'll figure he was making a meet with us, and they'll wait, and we'll drive right into it."

"He won't get caught," Brenda said. "He'll be there at eleven, and so will we."

"He can't be sure we even got the message," Ed insisted. "That's a pretty weird delivery system."

"I checked out of the room," Brenda reminded him. "He can find that out, and then he'll know I got my stuff."

"We're not copping his goddam money,

Brenda," Ed told her. "We'll call him in a week or two, make a meet, give him his half."

"He wants to meet tonight," Brenda said. "So we'll be there."

"*Why*, dammit? Why do a risk when we don't have to do a risk?"

"Because," Brenda said, "you'll meet him again. You'll work with him again. And he'll look at you, and what will he say? That's the stand-up guy came back for me? Or does he say, That's a guy I don't trust so much any more? What do you want him to say, Ed, next time you see each other?"

Ed leaned back, muttering to himself. After a minute, he shrugged, shook his head, and waved for the check.

The staff didn't think there was much hope for the relationship.

"I'll drive around the block twice," Ed told her, as they neared the neighborhood, "and if he doesn't show up, that's it."

"He doesn't know the *car*, Ed."

This was true. The car they had now was a black Honda from a side street near the restaurant where they'd had dinner. But Ed wasn't going to stop, and no argument. "I'm not gonna be a sitting duck," he said.

"There's a church, the next block, behind the

motel," Brenda told him. "Drop me there, drive somewhere else, come back in five minutes."

Ed clearly didn't like it, but Brenda wasn't going to change her mind, so he said, "All right, five minutes. But if he isn't there, we go. We don't wait."

"Naturally," Brenda said. "He put down eleven o'clock. He isn't there at eleven o'clock, we did our part, we go away."

"Sense at last," Ed said, and stopped in front of the church.

The quick way to the main road and the motel was through the small graveyard beside the church. Brenda went the long way around the block, and slowed as she approached the long brick motel building, with half a dozen cars parked at intervals in front of it. Traffic moved on the avenue, but she was the only pedestrian, and there were no cars parked along the curb. Come on, Parker, she thought, don't make me a dunce. I go back to Ed without you, he'll crow all the way to Baltimore.

She went past the motel office, walking slowly, just walking her dog, but without the dog, on this main traffic road where nobody walked. The office door opened and closed behind her, and she thought, hell. Dammit, goddamit, Ed, will you drive by now, please?

The voice behind her was smooth and non-threatening: "Miss? Just a second. Miss?"

She turned, and the guy facing her was in plainclothes, but he was a cop, all right. Big and burly, with an open raincoat and that arrogant smile. She said, "Yes?"

"Detective Lew Calavecci," the burly man said, and flashed a badge from a leather folder. "City police."

Be polite, be a civilian, be not afraid. "Yes?"

"Could I see some ID, Miss?"

Be a civilian, know your rights. Polite but firm, she said, "Why?"

He grinned, suddenly changing, as though he'd just remembered a dirty joke. "Come on now," he said. "I showed you mine, you show me yours."

"Of course I could," she said, wondering if a civilian would get indignant now, or scared, or what, "but I don't see—"

"Yeah, you're it," Detective Lew Calavecci said, and grinned all over his face.

Ed, where are you? Drive *by*, Ed. She said, "It? What do you mean, it?"

"Three men and a woman," Calavecci said. "When we finally listened to those other clowns. And the woman came *back* here and checked out. Nobody expected that. You play a tough game."

Indignant: "I don't know what you—"

Calavecci brought handcuffs out of his raincoat pocket. "Let's just see your wrists," he said.

"But— I don't—"

"You could turn and run," Calavecci told her, "and I'd wing you. I'd like that, relieve my feelings a little. Because I'm alone here, nobody could say it was excess force."

"Detective, please, I don't—"

"I *need* you," he said, with sudden passion. "They relieved me, sent me home, but I can still make it all right. I've had a tough day, I lost some . . . But *this* makes up for it, I was right, I knew they'd come back. You'd come back. Put out your goddam *wrists*."

"Lew!"

They both turned, and somebody was getting out of one of the cars parked nose-in along the front of the motel. "Lew, let me talk to you," he said, and straightened, and strode this way, and it was Parker.

Calavecci saw him, and his jaw dropped. "You! By God, *you're* a dead man!"

Calavecci dropped the handcuffs to the ground in his hurry to get at the gun in his shoulder holster. Parker was still too far away, but coming fast. Brenda lifted a leg, pulled off her shoe, and did a roundhouse right with it, the heel digging into the side of Calavecci's neck, missing the main veins but almost giving him a tracheotomy.

Calavecci yelled, slapping her away, yanking the shoe out of his neck. He threw the bloody shoe at her, gasping loudly, blood pumping over his collar, and he reached for his gun again as Parker got to him and put him down with two quick movements.

Brenda hopped around on one leg, getting the shoe back on, while Parker went to one knee and took Calavecci's wallet, badge and gun. Straightening, he said, "Where's Ed?"

Two cars had stopped out at the curb, wondering what was going on with the guy on the ground. Brenda said, "The church—"

Parker took her arm and hurried her away, back past the office, where the woman stood staring out, afraid to move. They went through the cemetery, dark and uneven but with just enough illumination from streetlights on both sides. Parker said, "Church. He's praying?"

"Probably," Brenda said.

As they came out to the next street, the Honda was just rolling down past the church. Brenda waved, and the Honda stopped, and they piled in, Brenda in front, Parker in back with the suitcases.

They drove down the street, and at the corner Ed turned right, away from the main road.

"We'll circle around," he said. "Then get out of here." He glanced in the mirror at Parker in the back seat. "You seen George?"

"Yes," Parker said.